TO HUNT A WOLF
BLACK MOON PACK, BOOK 1

HEATHER HILDENBRAND

BLACK
MOON
PACK

To Hunt A Wolf
Black Moon Pack #1
By Heather Hildenbrand
© 2022

All Rights Reserved. No part of this publication may be reproduced, distributed, or transmitted in any form by any means, including photocopying, recording, or other electronic or mechanical methods, without the prior written consent of the publisher.
This is a work of fiction. Names, characters, places, and incidents either are a product of the authors' imagination or used fictitiously. Any resemblance to actual persons, either living or dead, events, or locales is entirely coincidental.
This eBook is licensed for your personal enjoyment. This eBook may not be re-sold or given away to other people. If you would like to share this book with another person, please purchase an additional copy for each recipient. If you're reading this book and did not purchase it, or it was not purchased for your use only, then please return it and purchase your own copy. Thank you for respecting the hard work of the authors.

Paradise Cover Designs
Editing by Dawn Y & Tasha Lewis

CHAPTER
ONE

A dozen motorcycles are parked at the curb outside Inferno, each one painted with a fiery skull across the tank. The red and black gloss gleams underneath the flood lights. In this seedy part of town, nothing is sacred, but even out here where theft and vandalism are commonplace, no one touches the bikes. Not the ones with the skulls, anyway.

A lump forms in my throat as I study the painted emblem. Once upon a time, I rode shotgun on something very similar. Not anymore.

Never again.

Ignoring the pang in my chest, I scan the row again and then zero in on the one bike that matters. A black Harley with orange tassels hanging from the handlebars.

Bingo.

Looks like my mark has arrived, and that means it's show time. When I reach for the seat belt buckle, a dainty hand grabs my wrist with surprising strength.

"You don't have to do this."

I look over at my best friend, Kari, who sits in the driver's seat. Her curly brown hair is a mess after riding here with the windows down. Dark brown eyes that remind me of Bambi for all their innocence stare back at me.

I look away again, unable to hold her soft gaze. Inhaling, I note how her SUV is new enough to still smell like stiff leather; a gift from Daddy for her twentieth birthday. I don't know what that's like—no gifts for me and no Daddy either—but Kari's never made me feel weird about how much economic privilege separates us. She's the only person in our entire pack I call a friend. She gets me. And she never makes me feel cast aside, not like the others.

Not like him.

She's also my complete opposite. I am my mother's daughter—tough, fearless, and reckless enough for us both. Kari, on the other hand, is kind, caring, and way too trusting for her own good. In this moment, the divide between us is very obvious, and it has nothing to do with the fact that she's the only one of us who currently owns a car.

With her hand still gripping my wrist, she tries again.

"I mean it, Mac. Inferno's a cesspool. You really don't have to go in there." Her brown eyes are so wide and intense that they gleam in the street light we're parked under.

I shake my head at her, resigned. "You know I do."

"Is this about the money?" she asks. "Because I know you're saving up to travel but—"

"Who told you that?"

She softens. "You suck at keeping secrets from me, Mackenzie Quinn. I know you too well. And I saw your browsing history when I used your laptop to look up when the next season of Euphoria comes out." I sigh. *Busted.* "If you need money, you know you can just ask me—"

"Absolutely not," I tell her. "Besides, it's nothing. Just a fun getaway I was thinking of."

"You're a terrible liar." She flashes a rueful smile, but it turns sad. "I know you want out. And you deserve so much better than this pack has given you. You *should* go somewhere. Start over. Forget this pack of assholes who've done nothing but hurt you."

She stops short of saying his name, and I'm grateful. Even after three years, I can't bring myself to admit he's the reason I want to disappear. Besides, Kari's forgetting one important thing.

"You know I'm not going anywhere," I tell her. "Not without you."

She hesitates. "I can't just leave," she says quietly.

I scowl. "I know you still feel loyal to your father."

"He's a hard man, but he's my family—"

"Your brothers are your family too, and they would kill you if they could," I snap, but even after a thousand arguments just like this one, I can see her mind is still made up.

If she won't leave, neither will I.

I can't abandon my friend to the cruelty of her family. But I don't know how to save her from them either.

I lean back again. "Your father's offer included too many zeroes to pass up. And I need to provide for my future—wherever that takes me." There. I can at least admit that.

She scowls, her nose crinkling in disgust as she lets me go and stares out the windshield. "My dad's a dick for making you do this."

"First of all, even if I wanted to agree, I'm abstaining since talking bad about my alpha will get me locked up," I remind her, noting the current pack law prohibiting alpha-bashing. "And second, this is my job, Kar. So, yeah, I kind of have to do it."

"You could tell him the mark left town."

Her voice is so hopeful it makes my heart hurt.

Kari might be the alpha's daughter, but she's the sweetest, kindest person I've ever met. Kind of crazy considering her father is one of the cruelest. Then again, I'm definitely no innocent, either.

"If I do that," I tell her, "Your dad will just order me to leave town to chase him down."

Kari huffs.

Neither of us presses that idea. We both know my presence here is the only thing keeping Kari safe these days. Her family is Grade-A psycho-pants when it comes to hierarchy and inheritances. Kari is third in line for the alpha seat, but that hasn't stopped her two older brothers from threatening her life in order to keep their spots secure. Their lifelong obsession with stepping on one another to climb to the top has only gotten worse as we've gotten older. Kari's friends have deserted her. Except me. I'm just crazy enough to stay and stand between her and them.

Yeah, the Black Moon pack is kind of a shit show. We're complicated, dark-hearted bastards, every one of us. Except for maybe Kari. If we're the monsters who slither in the dark, she's dawn's light. Except, one of these days, even she won't be able to chase away the shadows that lie in wait.

On a sigh, I unclip my seat belt and reach for the door handle.

"Mac, listen."

Kari's voice stopping me yet again elicits a groan. "I know, I know. You hate this," I say, but she shakes her head, her brown eyes pinched in worry.

"I do, but that's not what I was going to say. Listen, my dad's been weird lately. Angrier and grumpier than usual."

I snort. "That's saying a lot."

"I know. That's my point. Something's up. His security teams have been replaced twice in the last week."

"Why? Did something else happen? I mean other than..."

I can't bring myself to finish the sentence.

Kari's face falls, and I curse myself for being an idiot.

But she just shrugs and forces her gaze back to mine. "I don't know. But whatever's going on... Just keep your eyes open, okay?"

"Head on a swivel, got it."

She sighs. "I wish Vicki were here."

My chest pangs at her words.

If anyone else said that to me, I'd be offended. My mother's reputation as the best bounty hunter this side of the Mississippi leaves me as second best, no matter what I do. Growing up in her shadow wasn't exactly rainbows and unicorns. But on this, Kari and I agree. For once, I'd be happy to pass this job offer on to her instead. Except that we both know that wouldn't work.

"Your dad asked for me specifically," I remind her.

"Yeah." She tries—and fails—to give me a smile. Instead, it's a grimace. But I know she means it when she says, "That's because you're the best there is, Mac. Now go hunt bounty and stuff."

"Fine, but only because you asked nicely."

I grin as I climb out into the darkness. The air is cool. Early spring in the mountains has a sharpness to it that nips at my skin. My tank top and tight pants aren't just a costume to help me blend in; they're a staple of my wardrobe. Seriously, the day I show up in a dress is the day to check Hell for ice.

Propping the door with one hand, I turn to peer in at Kari. "Don't wait up, Mother."

She snorts and gives me the finger.

I shut the door and head for the club.

Behind me, I listen to Kari start her car and pull out of the lot. I don't exhale until I hear her make the turn onto the main road. Crigger would flip if he knew his precious princess came even this far with me. On this, we agree. Kari doesn't need to be involved in what I do.

Hell, I probably shouldn't be in this line of work either, but no one told my mom not to bring her kid on the job all these years, so here we are.

Inferno is a biker bar meets dive meets techno club. Except without the techno music. Instead, the owner, some biker chick named Rita, who apparently won the place in a poker game twenty years ago, only plays country music remixed to a dance beat.

The result is a weird mix of "my dog died but I'm going to shake my booty about it."

The bouncer at the door, a giant, hulking man in overalls—no shirt—

glares at me as I approach. His underarm hair is long enough to peek out from between his folded arms. Classy, dude.

"Got ID?" he says gruffly.

This close, I can already hear a George Strait club remix wafting out from inside. Cringing internally, I paste on a smile and hand over my ID.

He peers down at it.

"Mackenzie Montgomery. Name sounds familiar."

"I get that a lot."

He squints at me, and I note the lines at the corners of his eyes. "You related to Vicki Montgomery?"

"Depends. Are you going to let me in if I say yes?"

His gaze hardens. "You hunting tonight?"

I flash him my fiercest, most cunning smile and wink. "Does it matter? Long as it's not you."

He grunts then motions to the door. "You break anything, you pay for it. That's Rita's rules."

"Noted." I push past him and through the scarred door that is stained with things I would rather not identify or think too hard about. Wiping my hands on my pants, I let the door swing shut behind me and plant my feet so the force of the music doesn't knock me on my ass.

Rita loves her some bass.

The very walls pump and grind along to the beat.

It's impressive.

If it weren't paired with a crooning male vocalist desperate to win his lover back by explaining how pitiful he is without her.

I don't do love.

Or pity.

No one in my pack does.

So I guess that's irony for you considering there are nothing but Black Moon wolves here tonight.

When I've adjusted to the onslaught of sound and the dim lighting, I stalk slowly into the club's main room. There are two levels—the ground floor and one above it that's mostly just a balcony wrapped with a metal railing where people can watch the dancers below while getting their own groove on.

I pause along the wall and take it all in, using the moment to pull the ball cap from my back pocket and stuff it onto my head.

No one I recognize, though it wouldn't matter much if I did spot someone who knows me. Chances are, they wouldn't want to admit knowing me anyway. I'm not exactly Miss Popular among my pack. If my mother's reputation weren't enough, what Levi did to me all those years ago, the way I fell apart over it—it's something I've never recovered from. And it certainly never won me any friends.

"Oh, shit, it's Big Mac."

I stand corrected. Apparently, there is someone I know in here. Someone I really, really wish I didn't.

"Hilarious as always, Guy." I roll my eyes, but he's grinning like the stupid nickname is still just as funny as it was back in middle school. Guy is still just as immature, so I can see where he'd think so.

"You here to party, Big Mac? Because, I don't care if you're a Romantic, I'll party with you."

"Mac and Cheese!"

Before I can answer, another male swoops in, looping his arm around Guy's shoulders. Their movements are loose, fluid, like they've already had plenty to drink. Wolves tend to burn alcohol quickly, so these two must be really knocking them back for the effects to show like this.

"Lenny," I say, tensing at the sight of him and Guy together.

One of them alone I can handle. But both of them together have a knack for getting under my skin in a way that always leaves me miserable afterward. Maybe it's the fact that they were there—ground zero, front row seat—the day my life went to shit.

"You out here looking for a new mate?" Lenny asks, eyes gleaming with what is sure to be a joke at my expense.

"Nah, bro, she's a Romantic, remember?" Guy nudges him.

"I don't know, she looks like a Reject to me."

I ball my fists as the usual taunts are tossed at me. Their banter clearly amuses them, and I silently run through every curse word I know, willing them to get bored and give up.

Finally, they do.

"Rejects are what I do, Mac, don't forget that." Guy winks at me as he follows Lenny back to the dance floor.

I watch them go, breathing hard against the hollow pit in my stomach.

Fuck Levi Wild.

Fuck what he did to me.

And fuck those assholes for making me relive it every time I see them.

If it weren't for Kari, I would have left this town in my rear view long ago.

I refocus on the crowd, my eyes drawn upward mostly so I don't track Guy and Lenny as they retreat. The rope and duct tape I stashed out back earlier is meant for my mark but it can just as easily be used on them instead.

Let it go. They're not worth it.

From the balcony, catcalls are tossed out along with—is that? Yep, it is—a push-up bra. Red lace from the glimpse I get. It falls, disappearing among the dance floor crowd, and someone hoots like they've won a prize.

Gross.

But it's a successful distraction from the raging anger boiling my blood. My temper cools, and I shove all thoughts of Lenny and Guy aside.

My wolf hearing is on overdrive, thanks to the noise, but I force my senses to remain heightened and alert. Somewhere in this thirst trap is my mark, Dirk Fletcher.

Wanted for crimes against the alpha. Whatever that means.

The charge itself is a broad bucket Crigger gets to fill with anyone who talks shit about him.

Honestly, the guy could have just called Crigger an asshole to the wrong bar buddy. These days, our alpha doesn't need much of an excuse to come after anyone. Kari wasn't wrong. He's on a hair-trigger, and we all know why.

Jadick Clemons is missing.

The heir to the alpha's throne. Crigger's firstborn. His pride and joy.

Right.

Jadick is a lot of things, but "pride and joy" aren't on the list.

I don't care if he never comes back except that, until he's found, Crigger is going to make all our lives miserable as hell, mine included.

Maybe bringing Dirk in will win me some brownie points.

I almost snort out loud at the thought.

Crigger doesn't even know what brownie points are.

Still, if I don't bring Dirk in, there'll be hell to pay.

Better get it done.

I scan the club again, concentrating this time.

It doesn't take me long to spot him.

As predicted, thanks to the intel I was given, he's at the bar, clinging to a longneck bottle. I watch from the shadows for several minutes, assessing. The crowd is older in this place. I'm probably the youngest by a decade. No one my age parties at Inferno—well, except for my high school bullies evidently—so it makes sense the bouncer recognized my mother's name. Most of these people will too.

I have to be careful.

Do this right.

My brain thrives on strategy and logic, and the next five minutes go by with me calculating possible exit points, counter-attacks, and contingencies. Every single scenario I run ends with me dragging Dirk's ass to the meeting point Crigger instructed. Though, one stands out as easier than the others. Fewer potential casualties.

The place is packed by the time I make my move—perfect for blending into the shadows. I weave in and out, head down. No one stops me. In my dark jeans and ball cap, I'm not eye-catching enough to become a target. Not with so many scantily clad women to choose from instead. I make it through the crowd with only two ass-grabs to my name. My wolf rears up at them both, pissed as hell and gunning for revenge, but I force her back down again.

Teaching these assholes a lesson about consent is not on the agenda for tonight.

Another time.

At the bar, a woman in a leather vest cackles loudly at something her friend says and leans into him. I use the opening to slide in between her and Dirk, deftly pulling my cap off and tucking it into my back pocket.

Despite the anticipation of what's to come—or what could happen if I'm caught—my heart thuds at a steady rhythm. My tendency for adrenaline, or worse, fear, died a long time ago. A drunk dissident at a bar isn't nearly enough to make me sweat anymore.

"Hey."

My voice is quiet against the chaos and noise, but in a club full of wolf shifters, it's enough.

"Hey, yourself, darlin'." Dirk's eyes are glassy and unfocused, but he manages to leer at me.

Perfect.

I lean in. Just a bit. Barely anything at all, really. Then I flutter my lashes. "Can you tell me where the bathroom is?"

Disappointment clouds his eyes. Then they spark again with exactly what I expected from a guy like him. "Kinda loud in here. How about I show ya?"

I nod, and he gets up from his stool, but not before he drains the rest of his beer. Waste not, want not, I guess.

Dirk leads the way, pushing through the bodies that stand between us and his destination. I quickly realize he is not, in fact, taking me to the bathroom. Mostly evidenced by the fact that we've already passed the doors marked with the restroom signs. He doesn't even try to hide the fact, either. Like he thinks I won't notice. He's either stupid or drunk—or both.

Finally, at the very back of the darkest hallway, he pushes through an unmarked door.

Night air washes over my skin, and I shake my head at the utter predictability. Not to mention the audacity. Don't get me wrong, I expect nothing less from Black Moon scum, but seriously? Is chivalry really this fucking dead?

The door shuts behind us, and Dirk whirls on me.

I widen my eyes and let my lips part in feigned surprise.

"Um, I think we took a wrong turn," I say.

Dirk offers what I think is supposed to be a disarming smile.

"Sweetheart, if this is wrong, I don't want to be right."

He sidles closer, and I back away, both of us doing this creepy dance until my back hits the club wall. When I can't go any farther, I hold my breath to keep from smelling him. Beer. Old cigarettes. And body odor that could peel walls.

Crigger really owes me for this.

"You ain't been here before, have you?" Dirk asks.

"Nope."

I shove the word out while trying not to let the stench in.

"Well, then, let me give you a proper Inferno welcome."

He leans in, and my knee slams hard into his groin.

"Argh." He doubles over.

I wrench away, mostly to avoid actual physical contact with the smelly parts of him, and bring my fist down on his back, sending him to the ground at my feet.

He sputters and groans, completely focused on his throbbing balls.

That makes one of us.

"What the fuck," he spits when he finds use of his voice.

I stand over him, a little disappointed he was so easy to take down.

"You were really going to force yourself on me, weren't you?"

When he looks up at me, I use my heel to shove him back down again. My eyes catch on the dumpster in the corner.

"Trash like you deserves to be taken out," I tell him. "Unfortunately for you, it's not going to be that simple. Come on." I nudge him. "On your feet, Dirk."

His eyes widen, and he peers up at me, hands still cupped around the goods. "How do you know my name?"

A bit of indignation—and maybe worry—creeps into his pained voice.

"Because unlike you, I do my homework on a mark before trying to drag them off and trying to assault them."

His eyes narrow, and I can't help but goad him. Any asshole who hurts women deserves a lot worse than a kick in the balls.

"I know several things about you, Dirk Fletcher of seven-forty-one Wichita Road, member of the Hellions biker club since age sixteen." At my words, he backs away, on all fours now. I let him. He's not going anywhere. "In fact," I add, "I know something you don't."

He glares up at me. "Yeah, and what's that?"

"There's a bounty on your head, Dirk. A pretty penny, too, which makes me wonder what in the hell you did to piss Crigger off so badly."

His expression twists. Anger. Righteous disbelief.

He realizes what I am; why I'm here.

Except judging from the look in his eye, he thinks I'm incapable of doing it.

"Fuck Crigger, and fuck you, girl. You won't take me in. And you're going to regret ever trying."

He thinks I don't see the shadow on my left, but I do.

A blur of movement. A silent attack.

Dirk's friends are fast, but I'm faster.

One, two, three; I put down the trio of Dirk supporters just as quickly as I did him. In the chaos, Dirk tries to make a run for it, but I drop his friends and then slide in front of him, blocking his exit.

His eyes are wide now, full of real fear.

"What are you going to do with me?" he asks.

"Well, I'm not going to do what you were going to do to me," I say dryly.

It takes me all of two minutes to knock Dirk on his ass again, and this time, I restrain him. He fights me, but it doesn't change anything. He still ends up as my prisoner. And his Hellion friends are still useless to stop me.

When I'm done, Dirk struggles against the ropes I bound him with like his life depends on it. Considering the mood I'm in, it kind of does. I finish him off by pressing a rectangle piece of duct tape over his mouth and then straightening. He looks up at me from where he's slouched against the dumpster.

"Mmorfghoh."

I roll my eyes at his attempt to talk through the tape.

"No questions until the end of the show," I tell him.

His three Hellion buddies are lying around us in varying states of consciousness. My right ribs still sting from the brass knuckles the last guy surprised me with. I nearly shifted right then, but in the end, my wolf wasn't necessary. I took these assholes down while on two legs like my mom taught me.

Four drifters for the price of one.

But I don't bother with Dirk's friends. Crigger doesn't care about them, so neither do I.

Dirk doesn't go willingly, though, and it's honestly more exhausting to drag his ass to the back of the alley than it was to fight him and all three of his biker gang friends.

Finally, I make it to the warehouse door.

It's non-descript and half-covered up with trash, old boxes, and a scrap of drywall beginning to blacken with mold. The area looks deserted at best. Dangerous at worst. We're close enough to Inferno to still hear a low hum of music, mostly bass. It covers any small sounds, including my footsteps and Dirk's muffled pleas. But underneath the music is a stillness that leaves an eerie chill in its wake. Nothing else moves. Nothing else even breathes in this place. Whether it's from the awful music or the sense of death hanging about, not even the rats come back this far.

This is why Crigger picked it.

No one will look for him here.

And that means, if this goes badly, no one will look for me.

A dramatic thought, but our alpha isn't exactly known for level thinking. And with Jadick missing and the fact that he requested me specifically for this job, I can't help but think there's more to this than just a shit-talking biker with a warrant.

I shove the door open, and it creaks on its hinges. Despite the inky darkness looming, my senses tell me what lies ahead is a large, empty space. Dirk's muffled attempts to cuss me out echo off the walls, the sound of his voice pinging back and forth only confirming my suspicions about the emptiness.

Somewhere in this old, forgotten warehouse is my alpha. And my payout.

My eyes slowly adjust, and I start forward.

I've gone several steps when a grunt sounds from deeper inside the space. It's followed quickly by a gasp and then a wet, gnashing sort of sound that makes me think of a blade scraping against bone.

I freeze.

Beside me, Dirk continues to struggle.

I punch him in the stomach hard enough to knock the wind from his lungs. In the ensuing quiet, I listen.

"You will not... get away with this... not this time."

The voice is pained and sharp—and fading.

It's Crigger, but not like I've ever heard before.

He sounds weak.

And very, very injured.

I drop Dirk, who is now wheezing, and race toward Crigger's voice.

As I run, a shoulder hits mine hard enough to make me stumble. The force of his body slamming into mine is enough to send me reeling, but it's more than that.

It's the scent.

I know that scent like I know my own reflection.

What it's doing—what *he's* doing—here now is a horrific question.

I catch myself and straighten, whirling toward the footsteps still racing away. They reach the door I came through a moment ago, and a figure steps into the opening.

He stops and looks back.

Behind me, Crigger's breathing is ragged and wet.

He's not going to make it. I don't need my wolf senses to tell me that. Death is all over this place. It's hovering over my alpha. And reflected back at me in the gaze still holding mine from the exit.

Levi fucking Wild himself.

Speak of the devil, and the devil shall appear.

"Mac," he says, and the pain that scrapes over his tongue as he says my name is like a brand against my soul. "What are you doing here?"

When I find my voice, the words that spill out are full of condemnation. "Did you just kill the alpha?"

"Mac," he says again, this time in defeat.

The sound of another door banging open drowns out whatever else Levi might have said. I jerk toward it just as bright spotlights click on to reveal a dozen men pouring into the space. They fan out, combing the area with flashlights and headlamps. One of them sees Crigger and shouts for the others.

Dread curls in my gut as their eyes land on me.

"Stop," one of them shouts.

"Don't move," commands another.

Even though I haven't.

"The alpha's down," announces a third.

One by one, they begin putting pieces together.

Crigger on the ground covered in his own blood.

Me standing here like a deer in headlights.

Another man bound and gagged at my feet.

I don't have time to process how bad this will be before a familiar figure walks in behind the security team.

Thiago Clemons, Crigger's youngest son. He's a year older than Kari and me, just far enough ahead that I mostly escaped his torture in high school. I've heard the stories, though, and they aren't pretty. Not to mention everything Kari has told me. His cruel eyes assess the scene faster than the others. Not a shred of emotion registers on his stony face as he studies his father's now lifeless body.

"Is he dead?" Thiago asks.

"Yes, sir." The security agent who answers him manages to sound sad.

Thiago doesn't react to the news that his own father has just been murdered. His eyes rake me over, and he snaps at the men closest to him.

"Take her into custody," he tells them.

Fear grips me.

This is bad. Like really, horribly, life-threatening bad.

"It wasn't me," I say quickly. "It was…"

When I look back, Levi is gone.

CHAPTER TWO

My wrists are bound—painfully tight—and before they even attempt to move me, I'm force-fed a strong concoction of wolfsbane to mute my wolf. I swallow if only to keep from choking. The deadly herb lacing the cold brew burns my throat. I fight panic, thinking of all the people who've overdosed and died from this stuff. But there's no stopping the liquid being poured into my mouth. When the cup is empty, I cough as my wolf strains to the surface one last time. She knows she's about to disappear, and she's pissed as hell about it. A snarl rips from me, and I lurch toward the guard. He responds by backhanding my cheek hard enough to drive my entire body sideways.

Pain explodes behind my cheekbone, radiating through my skull. It takes everything in me to remain upright and to keep from retaliating.

Instead, I bite my lip until I taste blood.

When I look back at the asshole, he smirks, which

nearly shatters my control. But then he moves aside as Thiago comes to stand before me.

"Mackenzie Quinn, notorious bounty hunter," he drawls. "Oh, wait. That's your whore of a mother I'm thinking of."

I don't even think; I simply act.

My skull cracks his as I head-butt the bastard.

"Ugh." He groans in pain and backs away.

Unfortunately, the guard is back again, delivering one of his signature backhands. This time, I go down on one knee from the force of it.

Not good enough, apparently.

Thiago is there in an instant, recovered and way too pissed for my own safety. He shoves me to the ground with his boot and delivers a kick to my ribs that brings tears to my eyes.

From this angle, I can clearly see the door I used to enter. The one Levi fled through.

It's empty.

Just like my stupid heart where he's concerned.

Asshole.

Just like the rest of them.

"What the hell do we have here?"

The sound of Thiago's voice draws me back, and I twist my head around to see him standing over Dirk.

Shit.

I forgot about him.

Dirk's eyes go wide as he stares up at Thiago.

"What is this, little Quinn?" Thiago snaps at me.

He doesn't take his eyes off Dirk this time, which is

fine by me. I'll answer his question if it means his focus is on something besides breaking my ribs.

"Your dad put out a bounty on his head," I say, the words scratchy and laced with pain. Behind my back, I work the ropes around my wrist, hoping to loosen them.

"For what?" Thiago demands.

"The order said 'crimes against the alpha.' That's all I know."

Thiago reaches down and yanks the duct tape from Dirk's mouth. Dirk chirps in pain then falls silent. He's not as stupid as he looks, I guess.

"What did you do to piss off my father?" Thiago asks him.

"I-I don't know."

Thiago hooks his thumb at me. "What about her?"

"Sir?"

Thiago rolls his eyes. "Did she kill the alpha?"

He over-enunciates each word, and I have to fight not to roll my eyes.

Dirk's eyes flash to mine, and in that split second, I know what he's about to do. He's about to screw me in the only way he can. And there's not a damn thing I can do about it.

"Yeah, she killed him," Dirk says.

"Liar," I scream, kicking my legs and trying to shuffle my way close enough to kick his balls into his asshole.

Thiago straightens and motions to the guards. One of them comes forward and jams a piece of cloth into my mouth. Another slips a black hood over my head. I begin to struggle. And then, something cracks sharply against my skull, and I'm out like a light.

THE FIRST THOUGHT I have upon waking is: Thiago is a dick. Not that I'm surprised. He's been nothing but a bully his entire life, especially to Kari. In that respect, nothing has changed since the last time I saw him back in high school, except that he's maybe worse now than he was then. Worse because, with Crigger dead and Jadick missing, he's now the reigning alpha of the Black Moon Pack. And that means he no longer has to answer to anyone.

I, however, must answer to him.

And he's given me the migraine of all migraines to remind me of that.

I breathe deeply then instantly regret it as my ribs scream in protest. Shallow breaths then. I take them slowly, listening intently to a steady dripping of water from somewhere I can't see. There are no lights back here where they've stowed me. Across the narrow space, I spot a dim lamp, but it doesn't offer much of a view beyond concrete walls. I inhale a damp, musty scent.

My instincts tell me I'm in a basement. Without my wolf senses, I have no idea which basement. Hell, I could be in another town, for all I know. But something tells me Thiago wouldn't let me get that far from his reach.

I don't have to wait long before he comes for me.

With my head still pounding, I manage to stand inside the small cell. My muscles ache and protest every move I make. Without access to my wolf, I won't heal any quicker than a human would. It also means my chances of fighting my way out of here are slim to none.

I'm at the mercy of a man-child who tortures squirrels in his spare time. Or, at least, that's what Kari told me once when we were kids.

"Good, you're up."

Thiago's eye twitches as he stops outside the bars of my cell. It isn't from nerves, though, judging from the twinkle in his eye. He looks excited. Like he's been waiting for this moment for a long time. The excitement scares me more than his anger would have. He has something up his sleeve.

Thiago watches me as if he's reading my thoughts.

I let my disgust and hate twist my expression.

Read that, asshole.

"Dirk had some interesting things to say while you napped."

Nap. Right.

My eyes track his hands as he pulls a rag from his back pocket and wipes his fingers on it. The fabric is stained red. My stomach knots.

"I didn't kill the alpha," I say.

"Dirk says otherwise."

"Dirk is lying so he won't be brought up on his own charges."

It's a classic maneuver on Dirk's part. Cliché even. But either Thiago doesn't see it, or he doesn't care.

The slow-curling smile he offers tells me it's the latter.

"Prove it, little Quinn."

His voice is velvety soft. A challenge. A dare. The look in his eye tells me he knows I can't.

"The pack is in mourning," he adds. "They're devastated over the loss of their alpha and demanding justice. What kind of alpha would I be if I denied them that? And with his murderer already in captivity?"

I glare at him, but fear slides beneath my skin.

"It wasn't me," I say, but we both know my words are hollow without proof.

"I see. And who was it then?"

I scowl, not offering an answer.

"I found you standing over his dead body. A Romantic with every reason to hate the man. Tell me, Mac, if you were in my position, what would you think?"

"I'd think I need to investigate," I say, but deep down, I can see his point.

I'm a reject with a broken heart. A Romantic, though I hate that label. I have motive, even though I'd never use it as a reason to kill in cold blood. That's not me, despite my rep or line of work.

Unfortunately, my rep and line of work are what make me a perfect killer. Thiago knows it, and I do too.

"The thing is, little Quinn. I'm in a tight spot here. On the one hand, vengeance must be had. On the other, you're Kari's best friend, and I know my little sister would be heartbroken if she had to watch you die publicly." He sighs like it's a real conundrum. Like he cares.

My veins burn with wolfsbane and rage.

His mention of Kari is a trigger. He's been cruel to her for years, always in secret. Always behind the back of his father. But now, there's no one to hide from, and that terrifies me more than my own fate.

"Leave Kari out of this," I say through clenched teeth.

Thiago smiles. Sort of. It's a dead kind of smile that turns my veins cold.

"Tell you what. You bring me who actually killed my father, and I'll let you live. For Kari."

I blink.

My surprise teeters dangerously close to relief before I realize what's happening. He believes me. Thiago knows I didn't kill his father. Otherwise, he'd never let me go. He's using me. Manipulating me to get what he really wants. I can't tell if what he wants is his father's killer—or me gone so he can mess with Kari unhindered.

"I'll give you a name," I say. "You can send your men to hunt him down."

"A name."

"Yes." My stomach twists even as I say it. The idea of selling Levi out is…horrific. But if I don't—what will Thiago do? "I saw the killer. He ran out right before your men stormed in. I'll give you his name. And you can let me go."

One glance at his hardened eyes and I know he's not going to go for it.

"A name is hardly a fair trade for your whole life, little Quinn."

"It is when I'm innocent," I shoot back.

Thiago glances back at where two of his security guards are stationed behind him. "Bring her in," Thiago says.

One of the men walks out and returns a moment later. In his grasp is Kari.

I grab the iron bars and hold tight, biting back a string of curses I already know will be pointless.

Kari growls at the guard. She struggles against him, but it's not enough.

He shoves her into the center of the room, and she stumbles to a stop beside Thiago.

"Hello, sister."

"Go fuck yourself."

"Oh, I have plenty of other options for that."

My hands tighten around the bars. "Stop this," I hiss.

"Mac?" Kari's eyes widen when she finally sees me.

My heart squeezes.

"What are you doing?" She aims the question at Thiago.

His eyes sparkle with an enjoyment that makes me want to cut them out of their sockets. "I thought you might want to attend this meeting since it involves your friend."

"Let her go, Thiago." Kari's voice is hard. She's trying to sound tough. But we both know she's nothing compared to Thiago. He's more than tough. He's cruel—and she can't match that cruelty. She doesn't have it in her.

"I was just about to do that." He turns back at me. "Right, Mac?"

I snarl at him.

"Mac, what's going on?"

Kari knows nothing is ever that simple with Thiago.

"They think I killed your dad," I say quietly.

"What?" She looks from me to Thiago. "That's bull shit. Mac would never—"

"He knows that," I say, and she falls silent.

I sigh, exhaustion setting in. I'm tired. And not just physically. Thiago has worn me down by bringing her here. And he knows it. "He says I can have my freedom if I hunt down the real killer."

"Then do it," Kari says.

I give her a look. "It's not that simple."

Her brows draw together in confusion. She doesn't understand, but she won't ask me. Not here. With him.

Thiago watches our silent exchange, somewhere between bored and impatient.

"Well, little Quinn? Do we have a deal? Or will you submit to the sentence your crime demands?"

"I…"

Kari looks away as if bracing herself for my refusal—and for what will happen after. I tell myself death is better than hunting the real killer. Levi Wild is a torture all his own. One I'd rather die than be subjected to a second time. The first time around was bad enough.

But I'm not inclined to explain that to my new alpha.

When I give my answer, I feel a little piece of my soul being chipped away. I'm honestly surprised there's any left at all by now.

"Fine," I tell him. "I'll hunt down the wolf who did this and bring him to you."

Triumph flashes across Thiago's face. Honestly, the fact that his expression registers anything but cruelty or amusement throws me off guard. But then he's snapping at his guards and moving aside.

The one who grabbed Kari earlier does so again.

"What the... get off me." She struggles, but he tightens his grip and drags her toward my cell. The second guard unlocks the door, and Kari is tossed inside with me.

"What are you doing?" I ask.

Kari reaches for me, but the guards are faster. They each take a wrist and pull me out of the cell. Thanks to the wolfsbane, I'm too weak to resist.

"Go," Thiago tells me as the cell door clangs shut behind me. Sealing my friend inside.

"Kari—"

"Will serve as insurance," Thiago says.

I stare at him in horror as every last piece of his twisted little plan finally falls into place for me. "You can't just lock her up. She's your sister."

"Return with the wolf who killed my father, and I'll let her go."

He doesn't wait for my answer before moving past me toward the door. The guards follow, dragging me with them.

"Wait," I say, desperation leaking into my usually steady voice. "You can't do this. She's an alpha-heir."

Thiago turns back, his thin mouth hinging in a calculating smile. "That's precisely why I'm doing it, little Quinn. Now, go hunt a wolf."

CHAPTER THREE

Thiago leaves my wrists bound as he marches me up the steps and out the front door of the alpha house. It doesn't matter that I do my best to fight his thugs or demand one last moment with Kari. My panicked threats go unanswered and ignored. Thiago has decided, and that is that. Even before he was alpha, there'd been no reasoning with him. Now? I dread to think what pack life will be with him leading us. Crigger was bad enough. Tough. Unrelenting. He expected everyone to fall in line. Thiago will be worse, of that I'm sure. Hell, considering he's just locked his own sister in a cage, he already is.

Outside, sunlight temporarily blinds me.

I falter, but the guard behind me shoves at my shoulders. I'm forced down the steps, nearly tripping as I try like hell to get my bearings.

A crowd yells at the sight of me, and I flinch.

What the hell?

One by one, all of their eyes fasten on me. I swallow hard, forcing my back straight and my shoulders down. This pack has already taken enough from me. I won't let it take my pride.

"Thank you for waiting patiently," Thiago calls in a loud voice.

He is unsurprised at the sight of them, which means he knew they'd be here, waiting, watching, thirsting for blood. No wonder he's determined to make an example out of me. One look at the angry faces and I understand. Our pack is in chaos over Crigger's death. Without someone to blame, Thiago's power is precarious.

"I've met with all eyewitnesses from the place my father's body was found," Thiago tells them. "We have a suspect. A Romantic, of course. This fringe group has become a threat that will be dealt with. Our pack remains committed to strength through rejection. That will not change. These Romantics will be found, and when they are, they will answer for what they've done. As one of them, Mackenzie Quinn has agreed to hunt down my father's killer and bring him back here so that justice, no vengeance, may be served."

The crowd makes noise.

Some cheer. Others shout demands. *Lock her up.*

Romantics will ruin us all.

Thiago ignores them all.

I can't decide if he's helping me or damning me to something worse by letting me go when they all so clearly think I did this. Then I remember Kari. This isn't about me. It's about clearing the way for Thiago to lead unchallenged. It doesn't matter that Kari would never want to take his spot. His fear is bigger than his brain. Bigger even than his ego. Definitely bigger than his dick.

He nods at my closest guard, and the man reaches over to cut the bindings on my wrists. They fall to the ground, and I resist the urge to rub at the sore skin left behind.

Thiago leans in, his voice low, as he tells me, "You will bring me my father's murderer, or Kari will die for it. Do you understand me?"

"She's innocent, and you know it."

He shrugs as if none of this matters to him. "She's a threat."

Not for the first time, I wonder briefly if he had something to do with Jadick's disappearance. The older sibling had been next in line for alpha. Not anymore.

My hands fist, and my lips part to bare teeth. Thiago's sharp eyes flick over me, missing nothing.

"One last thing," he says, turning back to the crowd. "Until she brings me my father's killer, Miss Quinn is exiled. This is our justice but not our vengeance. Not yet. I swear to deliver you both, in time. Your alpha has spoken."

The crowd goes wild, and I'm shoved down the remaining steps and into a black SUV. A burly driver waits inside. The second the door shuts behind me. The man hits the gas, and we speed away. Within moments, we've left behind my pack, my town, and any chance of saying a proper goodbye to anyone I actually love.

We make a right and then an immediate left. I know where we're going without having to ask; we're headed for the boundary line. On a lone stretch of highway, I stare out the window and let my mind wander back to the town we've left behind and what it thinks of me. Blackstone, Virginia started as a railroad town. That was two hundred years ago, and it hasn't changed much since. Still small, still simple, still trying to convince the outside world that we're merely human.

But we're not human. We're liars. Always have been. And maybe our lie is justified. Protect our kind from all the things humans would do to us if they knew we existed. I can sort of understand it, this "us versus them" mentality. But then came the cruel rejection of our own.

A century ago, our alpha rejected his true mate and decided, for whatever stupid reason, that rejection made him stronger. Others agreed—because who would contradict an alpha?—and the practice stuck. Toxic masculinity, werewolf edition. Now, our pack prides themselves on the practice of ignoring fate, hormones and instincts be damned.

Can a wolf die from rejecting its one true soul mate?
Yes.
Does my pack see that as a problem?
Not as long as you live.
The ones who wither away from their choice are deemed weak anyway, and who wants weaklings in their pack?

Not Crigger.

And certainly not Thiago.

There is power in being a Reject. And zero glory in being a Romantic. In fact, those who believe in actually choosing your true mate are cast out. And now, they're also being blamed for Crigger's death. It's a political stunt, nothing more. Because Levi is a lot of things, but romantic isn't one of them. I would know.

If there's one thing I know for sure, it's this: The Black Moon pack is as black-hearted as they come.

And now, I'm no longer welcome in it.

Exiled.

Homeless.

Inevitably, I think of my father, but I shove the thought away. Wherever he is, he's probably happy and definitely better off without me. My mother, on the other hand... I don't know what she'll do when she finds out what happened.

She's not a predictable person.

Vicki Quinn is a firecracker.

That's what the people in town say.

She always dismisses them, smiles in that way she has, and changes the subject. I don't press it. I already know what I need to know. Once, twenty-one years ago, my mom said screw it and had an affair with a human. They were together fourteen months. Then I was born, and she took me and ran away in the middle of the night.

To protect him.

As far as I know, it's the only selfless thing she's ever done.

She's going to raise hell when she finds out Thiago exiled me.

The only comforting thought that gives me is that maybe she'll find a way to free Kari in the process. I don't need my mother to help me. But I'd find a way to be grateful if she helped my friend.

The SUV brakes, and the momentum sends me shooting forward hard enough to snap me out of my own musings.

"This is it, kid."

The driver pulls over onto the gravel shoulder, and I glance around. We're in the middle of nowhere. Not that I expected anything less. I have no money. No phone. No car. And no chance of getting his help with any of those things if his expression is any clue.

Great.

When I don't move fast enough for his liking, the driver turns in his seat and pins me with a nasty look. "Did you hear me, girl? I said get out. Now."

"I'm going," I mutter.

"One more thing," he adds. "Anything happens to Thiago, and we all have orders to eliminate Kari."

I stare back at him, incredulous.

Sure, the threat is Thiago's style, but the fact that this asshole would follow through is asinine.

"She's next in line," I remind him, but he only shrugs.

"I take my orders from the alpha."

Our stare-down only lasts a moment before he's waving me out again. "Now get going," he snaps.

Arguing is pointless.

I open my door and climb out, sliding off the buttery leather until my boots hit the gravel. The door barely clicks shut behind me before the asshole hits the gas. He pulls a U-turn, kicking up gravel in his wake, then accelerates back onto the highway in a cloud of dust.

I put up an arm to shield my face from the rocks and dust.

When he's gone, I lower it and stare at the retreating taillights until they vanish into the distance.

Then, I'm alone.

The wind stirs the ends of my tangled hair, and I'm struck by just how long it's been since I showered.

The scent coming off me is…ripe.

It takes me a long moment to realize the fact that I can smell myself so clearly is significant.

Finally!

My wolf is back.

She returns slowly, stirring lazily against what remains of the wolfsbane. While my blood burns through the last of it, I start walking, urging my wolf to fully wake. In the meantime, I plan my next move.

Somewhere out there is a killer. And whether I like it or not, I have to find him and bring him back to Thiago.

Levi was something to me once. But then, he betrayed me and became nothing. After that, I swore I'd never have anything to do with him again.

Unfortunately, in a pack like mine, promises are made to be broken.

It's Levi for Kari.

That's the deal.

I don't even let myself think about it. I just shift and point my beast's nose into the wind.

It's time to hunt a wolf.

CHAPTER
FOUR

I hunt for three days before I catch a scent. It's long enough to fray my nerves over worrying about Kari. Twice, I retake my human form and find a phone, but the only number I know by heart is Kari's, and no one ever answers it. Until I can get my hands on Levi, there's nothing else I can do for Kari except keep going. Still, it shouldn't take this long to find him. My tracking power is better than anyone else I know, besides my mother, which means Levi's better at hiding than I gave him credit for.

Eventually, my hunting instincts win the battle and I catch a faint trace of him which sends me down the Blue Ridge into North Carolina. Lakeland, the sign says. Population a whopping 1402. The only bar in town, Quenched, has Levi's scent all over it. From the outside, the place looks like a complete shithole, which only makes me more certain I've come to the right place. This place feels made for people who want to be forgotten.

Only problem is I can't forget Levi. I've tried.

I wait for nightfall, using the hours in between to swipe clothes from a drying line in someone's backyard and trade a couple of hours of dish duty for a meal at some hole-in-the-wall barbecue joint. One perk of small towns is their willingness to trade for goods and services.

I'm tempted to work for another hour in exchange for making a call, but there's only one person left I know who'll pick up. The idea of talking to my mother is one I eventually dismiss. Even if she could find out if Kari's okay, I'm not sure she'd condone the deal I made. Vicki Quinn is all about looking out for number one; the exact opposite of what I'm doing by trying to save my friend.

In the end, I take the meal and forget the phone call.

By ten, Quenched is the place to be.

Its empty lot has filled with pickups and Harleys. I study the place from across the street, using my wolf senses to get a read on what I'll find inside. The door opens as a gray-bearded guy exits, and music spills out behind him.

Country.

And not the techno-shit they play at Inferno.

This is the classic kind. Patsy Cline, George Jones, and even some Johnny Cash.

I sigh but then immediately stiffen as a sense of awareness slams into me. I feel him before I see him. When my eyes finally catch up, my breath catches. A dark figure crosses the lot. His scent slams into me with the force of all the feelings I've spent three years burying.

Levi.

My chest tightens, making it hard to breathe, so I

glance away. My eyes narrow as I study the person beside him. The recognition brings with it more feelings I'd rather forget, but not in the same way Levi does. Tripp Thompson was my friend once—until he chose Levi over me. Still, the sight of him doesn't make me want to saw my leg off rather than walk in there and face him.

I watch as they both disappear inside.

Then I blow out the breath I've been holding.

I count to ten, but by the time I'm done, I still can't think of a reason not to do this.

All I can think of is Kari.

And Thiago.

And clearing my name.

So, in the end, even though I'd rather poke my eye with a sharp stick, I go inside.

The room is hazy, thanks to a cloud of cigarette smoke that's probably been hanging here since Patsy Cline released her debut album. My eyes scan quickly, and my hands are twitchy with the possibility of punching something. Or someone.

The bar is nearly full. Older men with beer guts. Some in leather. Most wearing the insignia of whichever motorcycle club they belong to. And one sniff tells me they're all human.

I relax at that.

Humans are easy.

Harmless.

I don't see Levi, but that's probably better. It means, hopefully, he doesn't see me yet either. Cautious, I make my way to an open space at the far end of the bar. Somehow, everyone manages to stare without actually making eye contact.

Par for the course in a town like this one, I guess.

The bartender sidles up. A woman whose years behind the bar have toughened her into a hardened shell judging from the no-bullshit look in her sharp eyes.

"What'll you have?" she asks. Not unfriendly, just impatient.

"Root beer," I tell her.

She doesn't even lift a brow as she turns away to pour my drink.

The sensation of a body pressing in close behind me has me gearing up for a sucker punch. Then I hear the voice.

"I thought I told you to lay off the hard stuff after last time."

Tripp.

Even before I've whirled to face him, I already know Tripp's expression will be fixed in a maddeningly charming smile. After ten years as friends, I know him well enough to predict his cheerful, teasing nature. Sure enough, his grin is the first thing I see when I look at him.

His boyish looks make him appear younger than twenty-one. That hasn't changed, I note. Neither has the shaggy hair he always insists on wearing long and unruly. He's my height, which puts us eye to eye. Great for punching, I think with a smirk.

"What the hell is a nice girl like you doing in a place like this?" he asks.

But I don't laugh. I can't.

"Tell me you're not here with *him*."

The words are out before I can stop them.

Tripp's expression twists. He rolls his eyes. "Don't start with me, Mac."

"Me? You're the traitor."

"You want to do this? Now?"

I bite my tongue to keep from delving into an old argument. But the pang in my heart is the same as always. After everything, Tripp remained friends with Levi instead of me—and that would always hurt.

"I need to talk to him," I say instead of beating a dead horse.

Tripp eyes me warily.

"Does this have anything to do with that trouble back home?"

I stare at him, not sure whether to pummel him or take his question seriously.

"If by trouble, you mean the part where I saw Levi murder Crigger, yeah, Tripp, it has to do with that." I dart a glance around the room, knowing full well Levi sent Tripp over here. Which means he's close.

I realize belatedly I've dropped my guard, and now I scramble to get it up again.

"You didn't see shit," Tripp says, and my hands ball into fists.

Behind me, the bartender says, "That'll be five-twenty-five."

"For a root beer?"

"Inflation," she says dryly.

"Here." Tripp takes a ten out of his wallet and tosses it onto the bar behind me. "My treat."

I open my mouth to argue with him, but the bartender snatches it up and walks off before I can say a word. Tripp looks back at me with a self-satisfied smirk.

"Levi went too far this time," I say, returning to the business at hand.

Besides, Tripp's already hurt me enough that I don't feel indebted to the guy for one soda.

"He's not going back, Mac."

"If that's what he thinks, he can tell me himself."

But Tripp doesn't move.

"Get out of my way, Tripp."

He looks at me, and I see something in his eye I don't like. Something that suggests he cares. Once, I would have believed him. Tripp and I grew up next door to each other. When my mom wasn't hauling me off to hunt criminals with her, I stayed at his house. We told each other our secrets. Helped each other learn to live in a pack that doesn't tolerate weakness. Now, he has Levi for those things. And I've been left behind.

I attempt to shove past him, but he grabs my wrist. "Mac," he says, his tone a warning. And somehow, an apology too, but I refuse to accept either one.

I wrench my arm from his grip and glare up at my former friend. "What are you, his bodyguard now?"

"He doesn't need a bodyguard, you know that." Tripp's voice is kind, which only pisses me off more. "He doesn't want to hurt you. Neither of us do—"

"A little late for that."

"But he's not going back."

I start to argue with him. Or maybe give in to the urge to punch him and satisfy the rage that's building in my veins. But the deep rumbling of an all too familiar voice stops me cold.

"Let her go, Tripp."

Tripp steps back, and my gaze collides with a pair of honey-brown eyes that are depthless in their secrets—and their wickedness. His hair is disheveled, same as it always has been. A windblown look that only adds to the air of danger that surrounds him. God, he looks even better than I remember.

I hate him for it.

And for the way my entire body reacts to him standing before me.

A fresh jolt of adrenaline spears through me, sending my heart rate into overdrive. I have zero doubt he picks up on my racing pulse, especially considering we're close enough to scent one another's dominant intent.

His pupils dilate, and a muscle ticks in his hardened jaw. He's tanned from what I assume is a lot of time outdoors. His muscles are lean though very evident through the thin t-shirt he wears. His strength isn't from any gym but from years' worth of hard labor and fighting his way through a pack who labeled him an outcast from the moment he was born into it.

We were similar that way.

Until we weren't.

At fifteen, I was the youngest in the pack to ever find my fated mate. Levi was sixteen, and he'd already had his share of girlfriends, but in his heart, he was a Romantic, just like his parents. We dated for three years, and back then, that felt like a lifetime.

Even without the mating call, I would have fallen for Levi Wild. But our pack thrives on the rejection, and in the end, that's exactly what Levi did to me. My senior year.

In front of our entire school.

"I reject you, Mac Quinn."

He'd spoken the words with enough intimacy that I still feel the sting of them three years later. He ripped my heart out with those words, mostly because I never saw them coming. In private, he'd told me he loved me. That our pack was stupid and cruel for rejecting their true mates. He'd told me we'd be the first to break the cycle. Change things for everyone. We were Romantics, and we wore it proudly.

But in the end, he'd become the exact thing he'd pretended to hate.

He'd broken his promise.

And he'd broken me too.

Despite my revulsion for him, my wolf and my own chemical makeup betray me. Standing before him now, the urge to go to him is a force, unlike anything I've ever felt. The need to wrap my arms around his neck, to run my hands through his thick dark hair, to press my lips to his—it's a desire I feel everywhere.

Patsy croons about it over the jukebox, giving a soundtrack to my torment.

"Hi, Mac," Levi says, the sound of his voice a sexy sort

of scraping that I feel right into the marrow of my bones. "It's good to see you."

"Bull shit," I say, but he doesn't flinch.

Out of the corner of my eye, Tripp looks worried. Levi ignores him. All of his attention is focused completely on me. It's stifling.

"Can we talk outside?" I say.

And even though he has to know my intentions are dark, he nods slowly. Every signal he's giving off is sinfully inviting, but I know better. Levi is at his most dangerous when he's thinking about sex. Or trying to make me think about sex.

He takes a full step back and gestures for me to go first. "After you."

"I don't think—" Tripp starts to protest, but Levi spares him a single glance that silences him.

I give Tripp a triumphant smirk, hopefully reminiscent of the one he gave me earlier when he tried to keep me from this moment. Then I shove past him and out the door.

My neck tingles with the danger, but I force my steps to remain measured and slow as I make my way outside. The moment I'm free of the stifling, smoky bar, I whirl.

Turning my back on Levi cut me to my core once.

I won't make the same mistake twice.

CHAPTER
FIVE

Tripp doesn't follow us outside. I can only assume he's found a different exit so he can watch from the shadows. He'd never hurt me, so I don't bother looking for him. Levi, however, watches me like a predator about to take down its prey. It's a look I know too well, and even now, three years later, it leaves an ache in my chest that won't quit.

"You shouldn't have come."

He doesn't say it with any concern for me. Probably just pissed I've interrupted his good time.

"Believe me, I wouldn't have bothered if I had a choice," I tell him.

Confusion flashes, hardening quickly into resolve.

"You don't belong here."

"On that, we agree. But you dragged me into this, and I can't let you just walk away," I tell him. "I saw what you did to Crigger. And Thiago—"

"Fuck Thiago."

I cross my arms, mostly to hide the fact that my nipples are hardening. Ugh. It seems three years without laying eyes on Levi hasn't been long enough for the girls. "I don't disagree with your sentiment, but I'm not here to talk shit about him either."

"Then why *are* you here, Mac?"

His voice becomes a rough purr, and I immediately distrust it. Almost as much as I distrust my body's reaction to it. To him.

"They think it was me," I say, and the fact that not an ounce of surprise flickers in his gorgeous honey eyes only enrages me further. "But, of course, you knew that already, didn't you? The moment you left me inside that warehouse, you knew I'd take the fall for what you did."

Something flashes in his eyes. There and gone too quick to name. "It's a little more complicated than that."

I shake my head. "Right. I guess it wasn't enough to reject me. You have to ruin my life too. Let me get executed for your crime so you won't ever have to see my face again."

His eyes widen, the barest hint of shock. "Executed? But there's no proof—and you had a witness."

"Are you kidding me? The witness you saw was a mark I was hauling in for a payout. You think he owed me a shred of loyalty?" Levi doesn't answer. "That piece of shit sold me out the moment he had his chance."

"You got out though." The hardness has left his voice. I pretend not to notice because, if I so much as scent pity, I will kill him right where he stands.

"Don't look so relieved. Thiago's in charge now, and he's not one for mercy. Or second chances. Can't say I disagree with him there." He looks away. "If you must know, I'm only here because I can't go back there."

His gaze swings sharply back to mine. "He exiled you?"

"Actually, first, he charged me with murder, which we both know comes with a death sentence. When a better opportunity presented itself, he decided to send me out here to haul your ass back. Give me a chance to prove my innocence."

"I can't go back," he says quietly.

"And give him a chance to lock Kari up instead," I add.

He grimaces, and I see true hatred flash in his amber eyes. "Fuck—"

"Thiago," I finish for him. "Yeah, I got that."

He levels me with a look that sends heat up my spine. "Did he… I mean when they brought you in— Did he hurt you…in that way?"

I hesitate.

Part of me wants to lie and say yes. Or at least spare him the satisfaction of an answer. But the tortured look he wears plays tricks on me, so I tell the truth if only to end this horrible dance we're doing right now.

"No."

He blows out a breath.

To my surprise, he doesn't seem satisfied though. His boots crunch over gravel as he wanders a few steps away to pace. I watch as he runs a hand through his dark hair, sending it into a messy disarray that only makes me want to be the one with fistfuls of his hair in my hands.

When he looks back at me, his eyes are bright.

"You could stay gone," he says. "Make a new life. It's not like Blackstone has anything for you to go back to—"

"He has Kari," I remind him.

"She's his sister," he scoffs. "He won't hurt her."

"You know that doesn't matter to him. He probably had something to do with Jadick's disappearance, and now he's going to do the same to Kari—and use me to do it."

He doesn't answer, but he doesn't look happy either.

I know before he speaks what his answer will be, so I'm not surprised when his shoulders slump and he shakes his head. "There are things you don't know, Mac. I can't explain, but... I can't let you take me in. This is bigger than you. Bigger than Kari."

Rage burns hot inside me.

I glare back at him. "You don't have to 'let' me do anything. If I want to take you in, that's what I'll do."

He faces off with me. An invitation. And a sad sort of challenge. But it's his pity that sends me over the edge.

I'm already tensing in anticipation when he adds, "You can try."

His attack is swift, but, more than anything, it's fierce. I stumble, narrowly avoiding the leg he sweeps out in an attempt to level me. Barely recovered, I swing on him—and am met with only empty air.

My grunt is the sound of my own failure, but Levi doesn't stop there. He comes at me again, offensive and defensive blurring into one move. One attack.

His body is beautiful and deadly as it tries to put me down.

Levi has spent his life training to fight, but his training wasn't official like mine. His skill comes from experience. A lifetime of fighting to survive—literally. The scrapping he did as a kid has made him cunning and limber, a deadly combination, and I hate him for all the reasons my wolf wants to take him to bed.

When he finally sweeps my feet out from under me, I don't know if it's because my wolf has decided to let him win or my heart is too broken to stop it.

I look up at him from where I've landed on my back. His expression is impossible to read, but I swear I see regret flash before his mouth settles into a hard line.

"You're out of your league, Mac. Go make a new life for yourself. You deserve to be happy."

His boots scuff against the loose gravel. Then he's gone, and my rage is a burning inferno that demands to reduce Levi Wild to nothing but ash—if only I could do the same to my feelings for him.

TRACKING LEVI IS USELESS. Not because I won't find him but because, when I do, we'll undoubtedly repeat the little song and dance from earlier. I'm not in the mood to end up on my back for that man a second time tonight. Especially because if it happens again, I might just drag him down on top of me and give us both a different kind of ending to our little reunion.

Instead, I find a shitty motel and break into an empty room for the night.

After a hot shower, I pull on a pair of black leggings and a sports bra I found at the gas station grocery store combo on my way over here. I don't love the idea of stealing, but without money or credit cards, I'm a bit strapped.

Pressing a towel to my wet hair, I eye the bedside telephone.

It's an olive green thing with a cord that looks stretched beyond its capabilities.

I wander over and pick it up, surprised to hear a dial tone.

Wondering if I'll regret it, I dial the number and wait.

She picks up on the fourth ring. "Yeah?"

"Mom?"

"Mac." There's relief in her voice, but I can already feel her breezing past that to the business side of things. "Where are you?"

"North Carolina. You heard what happened?"

"Yeah."

"I need you to find a way to get Kari out of there."

"Honey, you need to worry about yourself right now. If you don't bring back a body, it's your head—"

"I know, Mom."

She falls silent, and I know she's irritated I didn't let her finish the lecture.

"Who's the mark?" she asks finally.

I swallow hard, heart pounding. "No one I can't handle."

"I'll help you hunt if you need it—"

"I didn't call for help with the mark," I snap.

Her tone hardens. "I don't see how being angry with me will help your position. You're the one who got yourself into this mess, not me."

Her words slice at me, but I force myself to relax. "Thiago has Kari," I say as calmly as possible. "If we can get her out, I won't need to hunt the mark."

"Kari isn't my priority. Getting you off Thiago's radar is."

"She's *my* priority," I snap. Forcing myself to calm down, I try again. "Look, I called to tell you I'm safe and I've got it handled on my end. If there's anything you can do for Kari—"

"There isn't. Not without getting myself killed."

I bite back a slew of curses. "Fine. I guess there's no reason for this call."

"Mac," she begins.

"Bye, Mom." I hang up before she can start in on why it makes more sense to abandon Kari and save myself.

If she won't rescue my friend, I'll have to honor my bargain with Thiago. The only person who can help me now is Levi. And, like my mother, he refuses to do a single thing that would benefit anyone but himself.

Asshole.

I flop onto the creaky mattress and flip through channels on the TV until my eyelids begin to droop. It doesn't take long before I'm drifting; caught somewhere between awake and asleep.

It's a skill I learned as a kid. My mother's line of work demanded a level of alertness that left me with what is quite possibly a serious sleep disorder. Upside—I can be awake and asleep at the same time. Downside—I'm never under deep enough to feel fully rested. Thanks to a lifetime of this habit, I know with absolute certainty that sleep hangovers are a thing.

Tonight, however, I fall nearly into a full REM cycle. My brain begins to blend fiction and reality until my dreams are full of cries for help from Kari with a background soundtrack of Dance Moms reruns still playing from the motel television.

A scraping noise, so quiet it's nearly not there, wakes me suddenly. As a wolf, sensory instincts aren't something you can turn off even in dreamland, and my inner beast screams at me to haul ass. I force my body to remain still while I try to work out what's changed. A lifetime of training is the only reason I can tell when the air inside the small room changes subtly. Another body being added to the space.

My eyes spring open just as a knife is plunged toward my chest.

My wolf takes over, heightened reflexes kicking in, and I'm out of the bed and racing from the room before my heart has fully completed another beat.

A wolf scent slams into me.

It's unfamiliar. Male. Aggressive.

I catch a glimpse of his face, and while I don't recognize him, the knife he wields sends a clear message. I don't wait around to find out why the hell he's decided to try to kill me.

Instead, I run, and the fucker chases.

I make it down the short flight of metal stairs and across the lot before I know he's going to catch up. I can't outrun him, not on two legs anyway.

Dammit.

Woods beckon across the empty road, and I sprint for the cover of the trees. The moment I'm inside, I shift. My newly pilfered clothing shreds right off my body as my human form bends and breaks itself into my wolf. I land on four paws and shove off again, sending dirt and leaves spraying out behind me as I haul ass for safety.

My breaths are short, my lungs burning, and still, the asshole is on my heels. I feel the moment he shifts, and the air around me changes to accommodate his new form.

He eats up the distance between us like it's nothing. And he never wavers, not even when I manage to duck around a thicket to throw him off. Somehow, he can sense where I've gone even without the benefit of sight.

Tracker.

My senses scream at me, and I curse myself for being so stupid. I should have known. And if he's a tracker, running is the worst thing I could have done. It's only stirred his bloodlust.

Without warning, I turn and face him. He's close enough to slam into me when I do. I use my claws, my teeth, and my lean, lithe body to my advantage and send him careening sideways.

Mostly, it's the element of surprise working in my

favor because, as soon as he recovers, I realize fighting is almost as risky as running.

He's a dark wolf with sinewy muscles pulled taut over thinning fur. Patches are missing, and scars are evident in what looks like a body worn down from years of doing exactly what he's trying to do to me now.

Whoever he is, he's done this before.

Track. Kill. Repeat.

He's worse than a bounty hunter.

He's a hired murderer.

Where I stick to wanted criminals, a tracker will kill even an innocent if the payout is there.

But who the hell hired him to kill me?

I don't have a chance to ask before he launches himself at me. The force of his heavier body knocks me down, and I don't have a chance to wriggle away before he's pinned me.

His massive paw slashes down my shoulder, ripping me open. It's a narrow gash that burns instantly, and I renew my desperate struggle to free myself enough to roll away.

He doesn't budge, and when he pulls back again, I can see myself reflected in his glowing eyes.

This is it then.

Exiled only to be hunted down and murdered.

I bare my teeth, determined to go out with an attitude, and brace myself for the final blow.

But it's a blow that never comes. Not for me, at least.

Instead, my attacker is shoved off me as another wolf slams into him.

I jump to my paws and get ready to finish the tracker off, but there's no need. His grunt turns to a sharp yelp and then falls abruptly silent.

I peer into the shadows until I see him.

The tracker lies on his side, half-buried in a pile of leaves. His throat is ripped open, and his eyes are lifeless, aimed at the wolf who just took him out like it was nothing.

I look from my would-be killer to the wolf who just saved me, and the recognition slams into me.

Levi.

He looks back at me through too-large wolf eyes, and the breath is sucked from my lungs. On two legs, he's a human-like god. On four, it's all I can do to keep my wolf from rolling right over onto her back and showing him the goods.

She's all his, and he knows it.

I hate him. And her.

I hate this.

Mates.

It's stupid and archaic and a relentless wanting that burns in my stomach.

Levi stares at me so long that I eventually look away.

The moment I do, I know that's what he was waiting for. My submission breaks the spell, and he saunters off. The idea that he's going to walk away like this was no big deal sparks my temper.

I don't think about it, I just shift back and march after him in the murky darkness.

"Hey," I call out sharply.

He doesn't stop.

"Hey!"

Finally, he turns back.

When he sees me standing before him, he shifts too. I realize way too late what a horrible idea it was to provoke him because my gaze is instantly drawn to his chiseled abs and the perfect "V" that points like an arrow on a treasure map to what he has to offer.

Fuck me...

Literally.

Levi clears his throat, and when my eyes whip back to his, he's watching me with an arched brow. I bite my lip, terrified I said that last part out loud.

"Mac," he prompts, sounding smug.

I inhale sharply, not sure when my body stopped doing that without being told. And I'm just about to demand all sorts of answers to important, non-sexual questions, but then his eyes lock onto something on my neck, and he marches closer.

"What the hell," he growls. "You're hurt."

He reaches for me, and the moment his fingers brush my skin, I flinch and step back. He drops his hand like he's been burned. Our eyes lock.

"You're bleeding."

His voice is gentle. Kind.

My eyes burn with hot tears. Grief.

Because I know he's not gentle or kind. But dammit, I wish he were.

When I don't answer, he reaches for me again.

I wrench away and step back, crossing my arms in an attempt to cover up.

"You saved me," I say like it's an accusation.

"Let me guess. You had him."

I narrow my eyes at his sarcastic tone.

"Why?" I demand.

"Why what?"

"Why bother to save my life when I'm the only witness to the fact that you killed our alpha?"

Levi's expression tightens. Even in the darkness, I can see the familiar lines that appear at the corners of his eyes and the way his mouth turns down into a subtle frown.

"I don't want you to die, Mac."

The words are soft, almost like he means them.

"I don't believe you."

He stares back at me, eyes glinting. "Did it even occur to you that maybe I didn't kill Crigger?"

"Why are you following me?" I ask, refusing to answer his question. Or even consider it, really. An innocent Levi presents all sorts of problems, starting with the fact that we're standing this close without a shred of clothes between us.

My nipples harden in response.

Lie.

They've been pebbled since the moment he looked at me.

"I think the response you're looking for is 'thank you.'"

His answering smirk snaps my control, and I slam my fist into his stomach. He grunts, doubling over and backing away. Probably smart. I cross my arms, content to watch him struggle.

"Thank you," I say sweetly.

He straightens and glares up at me. "Next time, I'll let him rip your throat out."

I flash him a winning smile—and then promptly pass out.

CHAPTER SIX

I wake to a burning sensation ripping through my chest. Gasping, I shoot up out of bed and then immediately regret the decision.

"Whoa, easy."

A pair of hands ease me back toward the mattress. Bleary-eyed, I look up at Tripp leaning over me. He meets my eyes and immediately frowns at whatever he sees in my expression. "Don't even think about punching me too, by the way. I'm *helping* you."

Helping?

My eyes flick around what looks like a hotel room. I'm lying in a queen bed covered with a floral duvet that has worn thin from use. On the cheap desk at the foot of the bed is a coffee maker along with a placard printed with the Wifi password. On my right, a sliding glass door leads onto a sunlit balcony—and standing at the railing, his back to me, is Levi.

At the sight of him, I lose all sense of physical pain in

my own body. All that exists is the pain he caused my heart. I feel it—and him—like a punch in the gut.

His shoulders are tense.

He's worried—I hate that I know that.

Just like I hate that I have the distinct urge to go to him and massage the tension away with my hands.

Obviously, I'm unwell.

I can't help the pang I feel at knowing Levi is right out there but Tripp is the one at my bedside, making sure I wake up.

With that in mind, I tear my eyes away, back to Tripp, who hovers, concern lining his forehead. Probably still worried I'll punch him.

"Where am I? What happened?"

Tripp sighs. "You don't remember anything?"

"If I did, I wouldn't be asking."

"Fair point." He cringes like he'd rather nurse me into a quiet death than explain any of this.

"I remember a tracker trying to kill me," I say, squinting as I force my memory to return. "And Levi," I say before Tripp can fill me in. "Dammit. He took the guy out before I could question him."

The reminder irritates me all over again.

Tripp's eyes narrow. "He saved your ass."

I shrug then wince as sharp pain shoots from my shoulder down into my chest. "Ugh. What the..."

I lift my hand toward the source of the pain. My fingers brush over what feels like a bandage, but Tripp slaps my hand away before I can be sure.

"Don't pull the bandage off," he warns.

"What happened?" I repeat.

"The tracker used poison," he says warily.

"Poison?"

"Rattlesnake venom. They sometimes soak their claws in it."

My eyes widen. "That shit is deadly."

"Exactly."

"That son of a... I'm going to kill him."

"Too late," Tripp reminds me.

"Well, I'm going to find out who sent him."

I toss the covers aside and kick a leg over the edge of the bed. I haven't even pressed my foot to the floor before Tripp is shoving me back again.

"Tripp, get the hell off me," I warn.

When he doesn't back off, my fight or flight instincts kick in, and my wolf rears up, losing her shit faster than I can control her. My hands shove out, pushing hard against my friend's shoulders, and Tripp flies backward, crashing into the desk chair.

The noise brings Levi running. I'm still not even on my feet before he basically tackles me back to the mattress again.

"Get ... off me," I say, breathless and furiously struggling against his vise-like grip.

This close, his scent hits me hard, and my wolf goes ape shit for an entirely different reason. I force myself to keep fighting him, but in reality, all I want to do is hold him down so he can't let me go until I'm done with his ass.

Actually, it's not his ass I'm focused on just now. It's his rock-hard arousal currently pressing into my thigh. I stop struggling and, in a completely humiliating move, press myself into him, arching my back slightly to increase the pressure.

Levi stills and then removes himself from me, standing over me with a dark look that says he'll knock me out if he has to.

Honestly, it might be best.

My cheeks flame hot at what a fool I've just made of myself.

"Let me go," I say with not nearly enough conviction.

"You're weak," he says, and it feels like an insult rather than a medical fact. "If you get up now, you'll kill yourself from exertion."

"What do you care?"

His eyes narrow. "I've just wasted half a day babysitting your ass and this is how you want to thank me? By dying?"

"Thank you for what? Killing the only lead I had for who ordered a hit on me?"

"I saved your fucking life, Mac."

He sounds angry now too. Good.

"You also endangered it by letting me take the fall for Crigger's murder, and don't think this makes us even for that."

"This is bull shit." He cuts a look toward Tripp. "Talk some sense into her."

"Me? What am I supposed to say to her?"

But Levi just heads for the door.

His ability to walk away from me only enrages me further, and I lose all sense of self-control or filter.

"Seriously," I say, working myself into a nice little tantrum now. "Why bother saving me when my being alive so clearly inconveniences you? I mean, if not for me, you'd get away with what you did to Crigger, and you wouldn't have the whole salty, rejected female thing to deal with. Seems like an easy out to me."

He stops, his hand on the knob. His shoulders are stiff, his spine straight. But there's something like defeat in his eyes when he turns back to me.

"You're the only thing that makes it worthwhile, Mac. You'll never believe it, but that doesn't make it any less true."

His words silence me. Not because I believe him but because I can't think of a comeback that doesn't sound stupid and heartsick. Because I want him to mean it so damn badly.

He looks at Tripp. "Take care of her. Then meet me at Jade's."

Jade's?

Who the fuck is Jade?

An image of a faceless woman flashes in my mind. Jealousy stabs through me, and I duck my head to hide my feelings. Levi's personal life is his own. He made that clear. Unfortunately, my wolf didn't get the memo. Neither did my heart.

"You owe me for this, man," Tripp tells him.

He snorts, glancing back at me one last time. "Oh, I'm already paying, believe me."

Levi's out the door and pulling it closed behind him just as I fling the bedside Bible at the back of his head.

CHAPTER
SEVEN

While we wait for my body to burn off the venom, Tripp doesn't let me out of his sight other than to shower and pee. Even then, he's at the door when I emerge. Clearly guarding against any attempted escape. But Levi was right. I'm weak. Too weak to make a run for it, at least for now.

"You hungry?" Tripp asks from where he's pulled a chair to the foot of the bed. He leans back, propping his feet on the wall so he can tip himself onto the back legs.

I don't miss the fact that he's blocking the exit.

"I could eat," I say grudgingly.

Tripp isn't bad as nursemaids go. The truth is I'm a shitty patient. Not that I'd ever admit it. For the last two hours, I've given him the silent treatment, but my stomach will no longer allow it. My insides are cramped with hunger.

Tripp orders food and then returns his attention to the episode of HGTV. It's the latest in a marathon, and I'm nearing my limit on how many times I can listen to these people complain about what they deem a "design flaw" in a house none of them had to pay for. If I have to watch one more housewife bitch about her first-world problems of a too-small dining room table, I'm going to let the poison take me.

"So, you work for Levi now?"

No answer. Tripp's trying to wait me out. Fine. But I'm way more stubborn than he is.

"Never figured you for much of a foot soldier," I add, knowing full well it's going to trigger my former friend way too hard to not ignore me.

But he merely cuts me a knowing glance. "That's the best you've got?"

"What are you talking about?"

"When you're bored, you pick fights. I haven't forgotten who you are, Mac."

I look away, cracking my neck side to side like I'm unaffected.

"Why are you so hell-bent on bringing him in, anyway?" Tripp asks.

I cut him a look because now I'm the one triggered. "He didn't tell you? Thiago's on a power trip."

He snorts. "When is he not?"

My eyes narrow. "This time, he's clearing the board of anyone who might threaten his newfound power. He's holding Kari hostage until I get back with someone he can make an example of for Crigger's death."

"Shit." All pretense vanishes from Tripp's expression.

He looks shocked but not for long. Finally, he shakes his head. "I'm sorry, Mac. That's gotta be hard."

"I can't abandon her."

"Of course not. I would never suggest it."

"Levi did."

He looks away, his expression clouded with secrets.

"What aren't you telling me, Tripp?"

He sighs. "That's an explanation we don't even have time for."

I gesture to the shitty hotel room and my bandaged chest. "I'm not going anywhere—as you've made perfectly clear."

His glare doesn't have enough bite for me to take seriously. "Has anyone ever told you how annoying you are when you want something?"

I smirk. "You mean besides you?"

His lips curve. "You don't listen to me."

"I don't listen to anyone."

"Yeah, no shit." His smile fades quickly.

I bite my tongue, hoping he's going to tell me something. Anything. Because one thing I know for sure is that Tripp holds secrets. Some of them are his, and some of them are Levi's. And maybe if I'm patient enough, he'll spill a few.

He blows out a puff of air. "Do you know why Levi rejected you?"

I look away. "Because he wanted to look strong for the pack," I say quietly. "Because it was more important to keep with tradition and be accepted than it was to be with me."

Tripp scoffs. "You're an idiot if you believe a word of that."

Irritation—and wounded pride—have me grinding my teeth together. "Fine, what's your version?"

"My *version*," he says emphatically, "aka the truth, is that he did it to protect you."

I stare at him for a full beat before tossing the words aside like the garbage they are. "How does breaking my heart and humiliating me protect me?"

Before he can give whatever bull shit answer he'd planned, his phone dings with a text. I wait while he reads it, watching the way his eyes lock in on the words on the screen. His mouth turns downward in the barest hint of a frown, and then he blinks, and it smooths away.

When he looks at me again, there's no trace of any emotion.

More secrets.

Except, he's better at hiding them. Three years ago, Tripp wouldn't have been able to hide his feelings from me. And he wouldn't have bothered to try either. He's changed. We both have.

"Is your master giving you orders again?"

I can't help but goad him. It's the only thing I have left in my arsenal; if I can't fight with my fists, I can attack with my words. And I have to fight somehow. Otherwise, all I have left is the hurt.

He glares back at me. "I don't have a master."

"The way you jump when Levi tells you to says otherwise."

"That wasn't Levi."

"Then who was it?"

He looks away. "None of your business."

"If it has something to do with killing Crigger, it's my business."

"Crigger dug his own grave."

I eye him. "He had help getting put in it though."

He doesn't answer.

"Did you help?" I ask when the silence stretches.

His eyes whip to mine. "Screw you, Mac. We might have lost touch, but you know who the hell I am. And I'm not a cold-blooded killer."

"Nothing cold about it," I say, but he's right. I don't really believe he had something to do with Crigger's death. The problem is, I don't know if I still believe Levi did either.

"What was Levi doing there that night?" I ask.

I don't actually expect an answer. Like everything else I've demanded to know, I fully expect him to ignore me or change the subject. I almost fall out of bed when he says, "They had a meeting."

A meeting with Crigger. What the hell for?

"What were they meeting about?"

He hesitates, but I'm pretty sure if he shuts down now, I will brave the venom and a slow death if only to get up and kick Tripp's ass.

"Jadick," he finally says.

I blink, my mind racing ahead with what the hell Jadick and Levi and Crigger have in common.

"What about him?" I ask.

Tripp's phone dings again, and a second later, there's a

knock on the door.

He rises quickly, his finger to his lips in a reminder to be quiet.

I roll my eyes. Someone just tried to kill me. As much as I hate being forced into this bed to recover, I'm not looking for a round two. So I don't plan on alerting anyone to my presence here.

I watch while he pads silently to the door and checks the peephole.

Satisfied, he opens the door and then closes it again, a bag of food in hand.

"Hungry?" he asks.

"You know me better than to even ask," I say, and he grins.

We dig into the food, and I proceed to eat just as much as Tripp does. He used to tease me about it until said teasing devolved into a wrestling match that, back then, wasn't an easy win for him. Eventually, sophomore year, he hit a growth spurt and finally managed to beat me, but I refuse to let him live down the fact that, for most of our childhood, I kicked his ass.

His eyes sparkle as he watches me devour my food, and I know he's thinking about all those fights just like I am.

"Don't you dare make a comment," I warn him. "I haven't eaten in two days."

"I wasn't going to say a word."

"Right."

"Here." He holds out two white pills.

"What are those?"

"It'll help with the pain."

I don't move to take them, and he rolls his eyes. "If we were going to kill you, we would have just left you in the woods, dumbass."

"Whatever." I take the pills and down them with the last of my soda. "Happy?"

"Thrilled."

We lapse back into silence for a while, but reruns of House Hunters aren't enough to distract me for long.

"Why was Levi meeting Crigger about Jadick?" I ask.

Tripp doesn't seem surprised by the question. He knows me too well to think I'd let it go.

"Crigger was hoping Levi could help find Jadick."

"Why would Levi help Crigger with a damn thing?" I snap.

The only person who hated Crigger more than me was Levi. That hate was part of the reason I'd easily believed he could kill the alpha himself. Seven years ago, Levi's parents vanished, and Levi's never stopped looking for them—or suspecting Crigger as the one behind their disappearance.

"That's a question for Levi."

Right. All that means is Tripp doesn't plan to explain.

I huff and lean back against the headboard, thoughts turning over and over with the bits and pieces Tripp has given me.

Crigger met with Levi right before he was due to meet with me. And Crigger was still alive when I got there. That meant if Levi didn't kill Crigger, he saw who did.

I had to find Levi again.

If I could shake the killer's name from him, I could hunt that person instead. Thiago wanted a killer. That's all that mattered to him. I hoped.

"Whatever you're thinking, don't."

Tripp's voice yanks me back to the present.

"I'm not thinking anything."

"Right." He snorts. "You're never not thinking anything."

"You're just pissed I always won at capture the flag back in high school."

He rolls his eyes. "You didn't beat me out of skill. You talk shit and get everyone mad enough to forget what they're supposed to be doing."

"Don't hate the player..." I laugh as he gives me the finger.

"How's your mom doing with all this?" he asks, and I don't bother to hide my distaste for his change in topic.

"She's pissed as usual."

"If we're lucky, she's already hunting Thiago and will have him taken out by morning."

"She's not pissed at Thiago. She's pissed at me."

A strange look crosses his face. "Why?"

"She thinks I should stop trying to hunt Levi."

"I don't disagree," he begins.

"She wants me to stop doing anything that might help save Kari. She says I should think about saving myself. That I should move on."

"Damn, Mac."

"You know how she is."

"She puts her own family first. I can't fault her for it."

"Well, I can," I say fiercely. "Kari is my family."

He doesn't say anything. Tripp has never liked Kari, and I've given up trying to figure out why. I used to think he was jealous, but the truth is, Tripp disliked her long before she and I became close. Besides, Tripp has never been like that; threatened by other people. We never let ourselves get caught up in that competition mentality. Not until he chose Levi over me, anyway.

"If it were you in that cell, I'd do the same thing," I say.

"Back at you," he says with zero hesitation.

I don't bother to tell him my mother would leave him to rot just like she plans on leaving Kari. Hell, she might even leave me if I'd been the one Thiago had locked away.

"My mom's not going to help," I say. "Levi's the only chance I have at clearing my name and freeing Kari."

"You really think Thiago is going to release her?" Tripp shakes his head.

"He has to."

"Thiago's never going to keep his word. Even if you bring him Levi's head on a platter, he's not going to do something that doesn't serve him."

I hate that he's right. And that I have no other options but to deal with a man whose default setting is cruelty.

"I have to try."

"Levi's not going to let you take him," he says.

"I don't plan on giving him a choice."

Tripp doesn't respond.

I try not to think about what will happen if my friend decides to stand in my way on this. I don't want to fight

Tripp. But then, I don't want to turn Levi over to Thiago either.

The fact is, what I want no longer matters.

In the quiet, my full stomach makes me lethargic. Lazy. Or maybe that's the pain pills I took. I snuggle deeper underneath the covers. My injured shoulder stings with the movement, but it's not as bad as it was before.

"You hate him so much you'd turn him in to Thiago?"

The question is spoken softly, but my body reacts with a familiar pain in my chest, squeezing until it's hard to breathe.

"Don't try to make me feel bad about this," I snap. "Levi's the one who rejected *me*. He made his choice then. And he made it again the night he left me to take the fall for Crigger's murder. What happens now is simply a consequence of those choices."

When he speaks again, his voice is harder than I'm used to. It reminds me of Levi in that way.

"You don't know a damn thing about consequences, Mac."

I sit up a little straighter. "What is that supposed to mean?"

He's quiet for a long moment.

"Remember when Lacey Cartwright asked me to the spring formal freshman year?"

Okay, not the direction I expected him to go.

"Yeah. She was the only one brave enough to approach you. Everyone else thought you and I were together."

I almost smile at the old memory. Tripp and I have never dated. We played spin the bottle once in sixth grade, and when it was our turn to kiss, we both gagged and left the party rather than be forced to touch lips. There's not an ounce of attraction between us.

"Yeah, well, I told her no. Do you remember that?"

His humor is gone. He looks way too serious for some dumbass high school dance memory.

"No," I say. "I don't remember that. Why'd you tell her no? She was the prettiest girl in our class."

"Exactly."

"I don't—"

"Thiago wanted her. Everyone knew it. Even Lacey. And he'd already threatened anyone else who tried to date her."

"Thiago's a dick."

I hate quoting Levi but it's the truest response I can give.

"I still would have said yes," he goes on. "But that afternoon, Jadick found me in the locker room. He asked me to leave her alone. To not make her a target."

"Why would he have cared?"

"Because Lacey was his mate."

I stare back at him, sifting through memories faster now. Lacey Cartwright was the most popular girl in our class—until she was tragically killed in a boating accident the summer before senior year.

"Wait. Lacey was Jadick's fated mate? But Jadick never claimed her," I say.

"No, he didn't."

There's a lot to unpack in the way he says the word. Questions I don't even know how to ask.

"I don't understand. What does Jadick have to do with me hunting Levi down?"

"Jadick rejected Lacey."

"Yeah, and Levi rejected me. It's what this pack does. So what?"

"Sometimes, rejection is protection, Mac."

"Jadick rejected Lacey to protect her," I say, not quite sure whether I believe that. From what I know about Jadick, he's just as bad as Thiago.

Tripp merely shrugs.

"Okay, but Lacey died anyway. What the hell good did it do her in the end, to be rejected?"

His phone dings again. This time, he gives it his full attention and takes his time texting back. My patience threatens to snap, but even worse, I can feel the medicine really kicking in. Exhaustion washes over me, tugging at my eyelids.

I fight sleep, determined to get answers from this convoluted, bull shit story he's giving me.

I yawn.

"What does Lacey have to do with me, Tripp?"

He slides his phone away and looks back at where I've slumped hard against my pillow. "Hopefully nothing, kid. Hopefully nothing at all."

CHAPTER
EIGHT

I'm groggy when I wake again, thanks to the pain meds, but the moment I open my eyes, grogginess is gone, replaced by horror as my gaze lands on the figure currently standing in front of the glass doors. Dark blonde hair is tied up in a no-nonsense tail, and her narrow cheekbones are too much like mine to be denied. Strong arms and narrow shoulders are crossed over a lean figure whose slight stature hides a formidable foe or a very capable ally. Not that she has many of the latter. I still, wondering if I can pretend to sleep until forever. Anything to avoid...this.

I have no idea how I slept through her arrival or Tripp's departure. One thing I know for sure: I'm going to murder Tripp when I see him again.

She looks up from her phone and right at me—as if I've called her name. And maybe I have. Maybe she can hear my breathing change. The woman has the senses of an ethereal being. I almost snort at that. More like a demon. They're ethereal too, right?

"Hello, Mother," I say when our eyes meet.

Hers are a dark brown color that never wavers, either in color or aim. Mine are hazel—always changing with my mood. Like my father's. People say my mother and I look alike, though. The high, narrow cheekbones. Sharp nose. Full mouth. I hope we don't share similar facial expressions. Hers are much more venomous than anything I imagine myself capable of being. Like the one she's giving me now.

"Oh good, you're up," she says.

No relief. No, "*I was so worried.*" Just a clear agenda. My waking is one more thing to check off the list.

"Nice to see you too," I say dryly.

She ignores both my words and the sarcasm dripping from them.

"I brought you some things."

I follow her nod to a small bag on the floor near the wall.

When I look up again, she glances down at the bandages covering my shoulder. "Venom?" she asks.

"The tracker's claws were coated."

"And you haven't healed it yet?"

I grit my teeth. "My wolf was muted recently, courtesy of Thiago. My healing's still a bit slow."

"You always were prone to accidents," she says as if this is somehow my fault.

Instead of replying, I toss the covers aside and swing

my legs over. Unlike Tripp or Levi, my mother doesn't try to stop me.

My head spins for a minute then settles again. I'm faint. Weak. I probably need food and water and a couple of Aspirin. But I'll live.

Standing brings another wave of dizziness, but I push through.

There is no version of this where I remain in this tiny-ass room with my mother for company. Briefly, I wonder if Tripp called her simply because he knew it would get me moving again. Then I dismiss it. He's not that conniving.

Levi is.

I banish that thought too.

After finding and losing him twice now, I refuse to think about the man I'm supposed to be hunting.

When I can walk without swaying, when my mother's hot gaze isn't boring into the center of my back, I'll think of him then.

I snag the duffel bag by the wall and make it into the bathroom without further barbs traded. Just as I'm shutting the door behind me, I hear my mother call, "Don't take too long. We've got shit to do."

The door clicks shut, and I let the back of my head thud against it.

Deep breaths, Mac.

You faced down a tracker whose claws were laced with snake venom and survived.

You can survive her too.

I strip and stand in front of the mirror, waiting for the shower water to warm up behind me. I concentrate on the tape holding the gauze in place. With careful fingers, I peel it back from one side and study the skin underneath. It's already closed over with ugly scabs. A product of my wolf healing. But underneath the scabs and surrounding them, my skin is a disgusting shade of yellow.

The poison is going to take a bit longer to shake.

A smarter person would be resting.

Unfortunately, I don't have the luxury of rest.

The sting of ripping the bandage off makes me hiss. Tossing it aside, I look back at my reflection again.

My body isn't what I'd call beautiful. Strong, yes. But my hips aren't curved, and my breasts aren't full, and the tattoos I use to cover all my scars are a far cry from society's beauty standards. My fingertips trace my eyebrows, one then the other. They're sharp and angled like my face, little slashes over my hazel eyes that have a way of always making me look angry.

Or maybe I *am* always angry.

Like mother, like daughter.

On the other side of the door, I can hear her talking on the phone. Her voice is low, but I catch some of it anyway. Something about sending someone else. I'm surprised to realize she's being offered a job—and she's turning it down.

For the chance to babysit me.

Ugh.

Of all the ways Tripp could have sabotaged my plan to hunt him and Levi, this is the most underhanded of them all. I spend the rest of my time in the shower thinking up all the ways I plan to get him back for this.

When I'm done, I rifle through the bag and sigh.

The "things" my mother brought me leave a lot to be desired. The oldest shirt I own. A sleeveless, ripped thing I should have thrown out but it's the shirt I wore when I took down my first mark. Sentimental. Stupid. And the jeans are faded from wear and probably one good roundhouse kick away from shredding right off my body.

It's better than stolen leggings, I guess.

When I emerge, my mother tosses me a protein bar and a bottle of water. "Here," she says. "Take it on the road. We need to move."

I plant my feet, bracing for a fight. "I'm not going anywhere with you."

"Mac, now's not the time."

"Now's all I have," I toss back at her.

She rolls her eyes. "There's no need for dramatics."

"I haven't seen you in four months. And now you show up here and start tossing orders before I'm even out of bed. *That's* dramatic."

Her eyes narrow fractionally, and I know it's the only warning I'll get before she loses her temper. Most people are scared of a pushed-too-far Vicki Quinn. I'm not most people.

"It's been four months because I'm a working mother, and I will not apologize for that. Tripp called me because a tracker almost killed you," she says. "I came because you're my daughter. And now, we're going to find out who hired that asshole and why. And then we're going to kill them. Is that dramatic enough for you?"

I want to argue. To protest or put my foot down. To tell

her to leave me alone. But her plan is my plan. And with her help, we'll get answers faster. I'm not ashamed to admit that my mother has contacts that I don't. Forty-five years' worth of them. If anyone can find out who sent that prick, it's the woman standing before me.

I need her.

Doesn't mean I have to like it.

"Fine," I say, hauling my bag over my shoulder. "Nothing like a little mother-daughter murder spree to bond us."

Despite the bite in the air, we ride with the top down. After two days cooped up inside that hotel room, I close my eyes and tip my head back against the seat, enjoying the feel of the wind in my tangled hair. My mother's Jeep is a growly thing that's been everywhere she has. It's scarred and scratched—like us—and one of the few fond memories I have from my childhood. Sleeping in the backseat of this thing. Climbing mountains and boulders in search of criminals. Hiding on the floorboard while she tagged them. Then, later, when I was older—helping her take them down.

I've lived a lot of my life in this Jeep.

My mother glances over at me as we barrel down the highway. "You can stop trying to scent his trail. The rain has washed it away."

"I don't know what you're talking about."

"Yes, you do."

I scowl.

The woman's a mind-reader. And she's not wrong. Any trail I'd hoped to catch of Tripp or even Levi is gone with last night's rain. It's like even the weather has decided to take their side. I have no way of knowing whether I'm driving toward or away from wherever they've gone. But for now, I can't focus on that. Or them.

Right now, all I want to know is who the hell tried to kill me.

We drive west for two hours before my mother takes an exit for some place called Indigo Hills.

I've never been, but I've heard of it.

And what I've heard isn't good.

I cut my mother a look, arching a brow. "Mafia territory?"

"They trade in information and that's exactly what we need."

Twenty minutes later, the open road gives way to signs of civilization. Industrial buildings. Warehouses. And then, offices and skyscrapers. Somehow, out of the fields and farmlands, a metropolis has sprung to life. I stare, a little open-mouthed at the impossibility of this buzzing city existing in what was literally the middle of nowhere five minutes back.

"How in the hell...?"

"Indigo Hills," she points out.

I see them in the distance. Not hills. Mountains, really. They're such a deep purple, they look nearly black, and form an almost perfect ring around this valley. And around the entire city we're driving into.

"The mountains were spelled by the Crescent Coven three centuries ago. From the other side, the shadows play off the light, and it sends any would-be tourist or traveler right around them instead of through."

"How'd we get in?" I ask.

She smirks. "You have me. And I know things."

I roll my eyes. My mother's a little bit aware of what a badass she is.

We park in front of a skyscraper taller than any I've seen in this state, but instead of going inside, my mother leads us directly across the street to an Italian restaurant. It's a bit out of place, considering the casual, family vibe it puts out. Especially amid the glitz and glamour of what could have been the Upper East Side of New York.

I went there once.

Dragged a werewolf with a gambling debt all the way back to Blackstone. Mom tied him to the roof of the Jeep like he was luggage.

"Stay close, and don't speak," my mother says just before pushing through the restaurant doors.

A place called Altobello's.

The scent hits me first, and my stomach cramps. That protein bar is long gone, and this place smells straight up like heaven on a plate. At the same time my hunger hits, I also notice this place is completely empty except for a single occupied table in the back of the room.

Stale cigar smoke hangs in the air.

At the center of the haze, four men sit around what looks like a poker game.

Beers and poker chips litter the surface of the table.

Like they've been at this a while now.

There isn't a single employee in sight.

Two guards emerge from the shadows. One from the left, the other on my right. My mother tenses but otherwise doesn't react to the threat.

"I'm here to see Franco," she says with the kind of authority only Vicki Quinn possesses.

The security guard on the left grunts as if he's about to object, but one of the men at the back table speaks first.

"Vicki Quinn, aren't you a sight for sore eyes?"

His accent is notably Italian.

He stands, and I see that he's in a rumpled dress shirt and gray suit pants. Even disheveled, he has the look of a man with deep pockets—and a stomach for violence if the rumors are true. He's old enough to be my father. Or grandfather. But the way his eyes see everything at once gives me pause. I won't underestimate him.

He comes forward, arms open, and she goes to him, letting him hug her. She kisses both his cheeks—air kisses but it's still more affection than I've seen from her. Surprised by their familiarity, I pause a few steps from where she's joined him in the center of the room.

"It's good to see you, Franco," my mother says.

Not quite warm but not chilly either.

What a weird day it's turning out to be.

"It's been too long, darling," he tells her.

She steps out of his embrace but allows him to keep his hand on her lower back as they both turn to me.

"And who's this beauty?" he asks.

Behind him, the three men at the table look on with mild interest.

I meet his gaze. "I'm Mac," I say.

"She's my—"

"Apprentice," I say, cutting my mother off.

I try to hide my horror at the fact that she was about to divulge our familial connection. Rule one of our work is that we never, ever tell business associates that we're related. *You don't hand your enemy your greatest weakness, Mac.* That's what she always says. And now here she is breaking her own rule.

What the hell?

Who is this guy?

"Apprentice," Franco repeats, brows raised. I wait for him to point out the physical resemblance between my mother and I, but he doesn't. "And what can I do for you and your lovely *apprentice*?" he asks my mother.

The way his voice catches on the last word makes me want to roll my eyes.

Fine, lying was pointless.

Whatever.

"Can't I just stop by because I want to see an old friend?"

Franco laughs. It shakes his ample belly. "If only I could ever believe you to be the kind of woman who would do something so romantic."

My mother smirks. "You know me well, Franco."

"That I do." He laughs again. "Come. Sit. Are you hungry? What can I get you to drink?"

He leads my mother toward his table. The three men

make room. One of the guards pulls up a chair. I notice my mother's subtle wave at me to stay put. Fine by me. I do my best work by being underestimated and unnoticed.

Changing direction, I march to the bar and slide onto the last stool. The second security guard rounds the bar behind me, splitting my attention.

"What'll you have?" he asks.

He's young. Probably only a year or two older than me. Handsome too. If my wolf weren't mated...

But she is.

We are.

Dammit.

"What do you have to eat around here?" I ask.

If my mom can treat this place like a second home, it can't be that dangerous. And my stomach is painfully empty.

The guy smiles. "The best spaghetti and meatballs you've ever had."

"I'll take it. Biggest plate you've got."

His smile widens. "Coming right up."

He disappears through a narrow door along the back wall.

I refocus on my mother.

Franco is regaling her with some bull shit story about a high-stakes poker game he won. According to him, the pot involved a lot of money and a man they both knew who was wanted for embezzlement by some pack northeast of here. Franco took the man's money and made sure he was arrested by the end of the game. It's supposed to be funny, I guess.

She laughs when he laughs.

It's weird.

The guard brings me a plate of spaghetti that I have to admit *is* the best I've ever had. I stifle a groan of pleasure and honestly debate kissing him on the mouth in gratitude. Unfortunately, my mouth is only interested in kissing one person, and it's not this guy. Because that would be too easy; wanting someone who wants me back.

Ugh.

I wash the food down with water because, even though I'm pretty sure they won't poison me—I'm already poisoned, technically—I'm not stupid enough to lose my wits in a place like this.

The fact that it's empty at lunchtime speaks volumes about what these men are and what sort of business goes on in here.

"Franco, listen," my mom says as I polish off the last of my food. Finally, we're getting down to business. "I need to know what you've heard about a tracker hired for a contract liquidation."

"Hm. Was the liquidation successful?" Franco asks.

My mother's gaze flicks to me. "No."

"I see."

And I can tell by the sharpness in Franco's gaze that he does see.

"Now that you mention it, I did hear something about an inside hire."

I straighten in my seat.

My mother doesn't react.

"Inside hire?" she repeats with a practiced sort of curiosity.

"Your new alpha. What's his name?" Franco snaps his finger. "Theo?"

"Thiago." My voice rings out clearly across the room. The men all turn to look at me, and my mother glares.

I told you to stay quiet, her eyes scream.

I ignore her.

My stomach churns with rage. Thiago spared my life only to exile me and try to kill me once I'd left his borders. It doesn't make sense. But then, I think of Kari, and, actually, it makes perfect sense.

He only spared me as an excuse to get to her.

With me gone, he has no reason to release her.

Ever.

This was never about Crigger's killer, this was about Thiago eliminating his own competition.

My mother's anger is a frequency screeching in my head. But I don't let her rules keep me from getting my own answers. This is my fight just as much as hers. More, actually.

"Thiago Clemons. He's the new alpha of our pack," I say. "Is that who you mean?"

"Yes, Thiago. Crigger's kid." Franco studies me. "He's making a power play of it, from what I hear."

"He's a dick," I say, and the guard who fed me snickers from where he leans against the wall not far away.

"He's got a lot to prove and not a lot of time to prove it," Franco says.

"He paid the contract," my mother says. "You're sure of it?"

"I could be sure. Depends on what you've got for me."

I have no idea what my mother has for him. Or what he'll want. But she's unruffled.

"Marco Gerardo," she says smoothly.

Franco stares back at her. "You sure about that?"

He sounds deadly serious now. In fact, all three men at the table are leaning forward. Whoever Marco is, they seem very interested in him.

"I could be sure," my mother says. "If you are."

"I am," Franco says without hesitation. "Your alpha paid the contract."

My mother nods. "Marco's your guy." She pushes to her feet. "Come on, Mac. It's time to go."

Franco stands, and the two guards snap to attention, closing in so they flank him as he walks my mother to the door.

"Thanks," I tell the one who fed me.

"Anytime," he says, and I can hear the undercurrent of attraction.

He's flirting.

I want to flirt back. But something stops me. And it's not my heart's stupid relentless devotion to an asshole. Something else ties my tongue.

The mate call.

Alarm shoots through me as I realize Levi is here. With every ounce of self-control I possess, I keep my eyes trained on the guard as I smile tightly and then join my mother at the exit.

Franco says goodbye. My mother promises to "come by soon." And we leave. All the while, I'm hyper-aware of Levi's presence. Somewhere close by.

When we're back on the sidewalk, the feeling intensifies.

Still, I don't search for him.

I refuse to let him know I can sense him. Not until I know why he's here.

Whatever he's up to, he's not going to get away with it again.

CHAPTER NINE

The street is crowded with traffic. It takes us several minutes to cross to where Mom parked the Jeep. The entire time, I feel him nearby. Levi. He's above me, that much I know. But I don't look up to see exactly where.

My mom is clearly oblivious to it. She marches straight to the Jeep and unlocks it with her fob. But I hesitate.

"Where are we going now?"

"Not 'we,'" she corrects. "Just me."

"Excuse me?"

"You're going to find a safe place to lay low while I handle this."

"You can't be serious. You want me to *hide*?"

"I want you to *live*," she snaps then reaches for her door handle and yanks harder than necessary. She's pissed. And now that Franco isn't watching, she's letting it show.

But I don't move to open my door.

"Get in," she says.

"No."

"Mac," she warns. "We don't have time for this."

"You're going to kill him, aren't you?"

She doesn't even pretend to be confused about who I mean. We both know I'm talking about Thiago—the asshole who paid to have me killed.

"He messed with my family," is all she says.

Like that's all the reason she needs.

Maybe it is, but it's not a good enough reason to shove me in a hole somewhere while she does all the dirty work. The words of that security guard ring in my head. If something happens to Thiago, that would make Kari automatic alpha. Would he really carry out Thiago's order to kill her? I can't be sure, and the thought of risking it—of letting my mother loose on him—makes me sick.

"I won't be left behind on this."

"You'll do what I say until I make it safe for you again," she says.

Her voice is more than a warning now. It's a promise that she intends to get her way even if it means taking me by force.

"He has Kari," I remind her. "And he's threatened to hurt her if something happens to him. Do your plans include making sure she *doesn't* get hurt?"

"I'll do my best."

"Not good enough," I all but yell.

My mother hesitates. "You're my daughter, Mac." Desperation leaks into her eyes. "What am I supposed to do?"

Vulnerability is only there for a second, and then it's gone. The mask is back. But even a glimpse is proof she's more upset than I realized.

Still, I can't let her make a bigger mess of what's already a shitshow.

"I can't let you do this," I say.

Instead of giving in, though, her expression hardens. "It's not up to you."

When I still don't move, I expect her to come at me, maybe even physically put me in this car. She can try, anyway. I've never come to blows with my mother, but for this, for Kari, I would.

But instead, she pulls out her phone and dials a number.

"Tell Franco Mac is staying here until I get back," she says.

"What?" My eyes widen. No freaking way she's dumping me with the mafia while she kills Thiago.

"Yeah, I'll owe him," she says in response to whoever's on the other end of the call.

She hangs up and glances at me one last time. "I can't not protect you, Mac. You'll understand someday."

In the next second, she climbs into the car alone and starts the engine.

She engages the door locks.

Then she drives off.

My heart pounds as I try to think. Franco's going to lock me in a room if he gets his hands on me. Been there, done that. Not doing it again.

I whirl and catch sight of the two security guards

emerging from the restaurant. They search the sidewalk and street beyond until their eyes land on me standing in the middle of this parallel parking space.

They start for me, ignoring the crosswalk and the traffic, which somehow just knows enough to stop for them.

Shit.

Time to move.

I whirl and take off for the nearest alleyway at a full sprint.

My shoulder burns a little as the poison stirs in my blood now pumping faster than before. I don't stop or slow. And I don't worry about finding an exit. Instead, I follow the call of my mate.

Levi's already headed out, but I've still got a lock on him.

With any luck, he'll lead me away from these assholes and maybe even give me a chance to make good on my promise to haul his ass in. If I can get to Thiago before my mother, with Levi in custody, maybe I can still save Kari before shit hits the fan.

I run until my lungs burn and my chest threatens to cave in around the pain. Twice, I consider shifting, but there are too many people, and I'm sure a wolf in the city will be more noticeable than a strange girl. Even in a metropolis full of werewolves, there are rules about propriety.

Levi stays far enough ahead that I'm terrified I'll lose him at any moment. The only good thing about his superior speed is that I'm fairly certain he has no idea I'm following.

He finally stops when we reach the outskirts of town, at a retirement community complex of all places, and I hang back, catching my breath while I note the apartment he enters. At least I've lost Franco's men. For now.

The traffic is almost non-existent here, and while the neighborhood seems nice enough with the tiny manicured patches of grass and pretty white gate blocking access to non-residents, I can't help but feel a sense of eyes on the place.

I wait an hour, trying to assess what's going on behind closed doors. But Levi doesn't emerge, and no one else goes in or out of the place either. It's stupid to walk blindly into something like this, and if Levi were any other mark, I wouldn't do it. But staying out here is more of a risk considering the entire Indigo Hills Mafia is probably looking for me now.

I can either stay out here and wait for Franco and his guys to haul me in. Or I can use the element of surprise to apprehend Levi and trade him for Kari.

I head for the apartment, skipping the front gate and, instead, veering around the back.

Climbing the low wall, I dart between hedges until I'm right outside the apartment I watched Levi enter. It has a large front window covered in blinds. I bend low to bypass it and find a small fenced-in backyard around the side.

Scaling the fence, I drop to my feet on the other side and hurry to the back door.

Unlocked.

These guys are seriously sure of themselves.

I slide it open as silently as possible.

My shoulder burns. My heart pounds. My breaths are short and shallow, but I make sure to keep them silent as I walk through the back door and into a small kitchen.

A table and set of chairs sits between me and the rest of the house. My eyes land on a figure sitting at the table, and I stop cold. When I see who it is sitting before me, my jaw drops.

For a second, I forget all about Levi. Or Thiago. Or even Kari.

"Jadick?" I whisper.

My brain catches on the fact that I'm standing in the same room with our missing alpha-heir.

"Hello." His greeting is smooth and way too calm given I've just broken into his house.

"Holy shit."

Jadick Clemons is alive and well.

Shock is replaced by hope. The welling in my chest is overwhelming, and I don't know whether to laugh or cry or punch something. Namely him.

"You're alive," I blurt.

"That's a very astute observation."

My shock dissolves into fury.

"What the hell is the matter with you?" I demand. "Why are you hiding out here when your pack's fallen into the hands of your psychopath brother?"

"You must be Mac," he says in a deep voice that doesn't miss a beat, considering the accusations I've just spewed. "We've been expecting you."

Shit.

The realization I'm not as stealthy as I thought comes

three seconds before someone grabs me from behind and hauls me off my feet. Despite my attempt to run, I'm tossed over a very broad, very strong shoulder and held down by an arm that is muscled to perfection. An arm I'd lick if I had any less self-respect.

Levi.

His scent slams into me, and I realize belatedly the shock of seeing Jadick here has dulled my senses. I never even saw him coming.

Dammit.

"Put me down." I try to sound tough, but when you're slung over someone else's shoulder like a sack of potatoes, it's hard to sound scary or intimidating.

To make up for it, I fight, kicking wildly until my toe lands solidly against the parts of him I accidentally sex-dream about at night sometimes.

"Ugh." He grunts and almost drops me.

Almost.

But not quite. When he adjusts his grip, tighter than before, I know fighting isn't going to work. Out of sheer desperation, I play the only card I have left.

I lick his arm, self-respect be damned.

"Did you just ... lick me?"

"Damn right." I beat my fists against his back. "And there's more where that came from."

I'm pretty sure I hear Jadick snicker.

"She sounds like she means it," he says.

Levi sighs. "Mac, I swear, you're going to be the death of me."

He sounds mildly irritated, which is nothing compared

to how I feel about him leaving me in that hotel with Tripp—and then my mother.

Abandoning the licking, since it will only lead to me enjoying my current predicament, I try another tactic. With every ounce of momentum I have, I wrench myself sideways and succeed in falling off Levi's shoulder. I land on the kitchen floor—right on my face. Probably should have thought that through.

The tile is cold and hard against my cheek, and I wince at the pain shooting through my cheekbone. When I pry myself up again, a pair of boots steps into view about six inches from my eyeballs. I follow them upward until I see Tripp glaring down at me. Beside him, Levi is still cupping himself in pain. Whoops.

Behind him, Jadick sits at the table, watching us all with an amused expression.

"When you said she fights dirty, you weren't kidding," Jadick says.

Levi glares at him, which is good because I don't think I have it in me to do it myself right now. Tripp extends a hand to help me up, but I ignore it and climb to my feet, gritting my teeth at the pulsing pain in my face.

"Damn, girl." Tripp studies the damage I've done to myself. "You kicked your own ass."

"And his." I smirk at Levi, and Tripp tries and fails to keep from laughing.

"She's got you there," Tripp tells him.

"Lucky shot," Levi grumbles, trying to look recovered even though I'm sure it still hurts. After all, it's only been three years since I last had my hands on the goods, and that's not something a girl forgets. Not that I've fully experienced it, but our make-out sessions came close enough and—

"I think I saw a pack of peas in the freezer," Tripp says.

I shake off the urge to daydream about the size of Levi's dick. Right now, he's being one, and that's what matters.

"Does someone want to explain to me what the alpha-heir is doing in a retired living community on the edge of mafia territory?" I ask. "Or why he isn't currently taking his rightful place among our pack?"

"Not particularly," Levi says.

This time, I do actually manage to glare. "I think you owe me an explanation."

"Hey, you're the one who crashed our party," Tripp says to me. "You don't just get to demand answers too."

"He has a point," Jadick says, but he looks like he's enjoying all the banter more than he wants to be a hardass about anything. "Maybe you could start with an explanation of your own," he says to me. "Tell us what you're doing here, and maybe we'll do the same."

"Yeah." Tripp crosses his arms. "I, for one, would love to hear that story. And where's Vicki?"

"Oh, you mean the babysitter you called for me and then dipped out because you're too chickenshit to tell me you called my mother on me?"

"Uh-oh," Tripp says, and his smirk vanishes.

"I am going to kick your ass for that," I tell him.

Before he can offer an apology—or claim temporary insanity—there's a knock at the front door.

No, a pounding.

A fist bangs against the steel door so hard it shakes the entire apartment.

We all fall silent. Judging from the wide-eyed stares the guys are giving one another, they have no idea who it is. My stomach tightens because there's a very good chance I brought this trouble with me.

"Mackenzie Quinn," an unfamiliar voice shouts from outside.

Dammit.

Make that a one hundred percent chance.

"Any idea who that is?" Levi asks me.

"Umm, possibly the mafia?"

His expression darkens.

I wince.

The voice calls out again. "Come out, or we're coming in. We don't want trouble," the man adds, and I can't help but roll my eyes at that.

Riiight.

Because banging violently on a front door just screams *peace and love.*

"You led the mafia to our doorstep?" Tripp hisses. "While we're housing a fugitive? Are you insane?"

I give him a look that's somewhere between admitting that I'm an idiot and straight-up fear. "Whoops?"

Levi curses.

I can almost see the urge to wring my neck playing across his delicious features. The banging comes again, and he blinks like it's snapped him out of whatever daydream of my ass-whooping he just experienced.

"Take Jadick with you," he tells Tripp. "Go to Jade's."

The name reignites a flame of jealousy inside me. I glare at them all, not even caring if it shows at this point.

"What about you?" Tripp says.

Levi looks back at me, his expression blazing just as hot as my own. "Mac and I are going to have a little talk."

CHAPTER
TEN

I don't argue. Mostly because I have my own reasons for wanting to be alone with Levi. None of those ideas involve talking, especially the ones I've forbidden my hormones from attempting. But mostly, I recognize this as my chance to finally apprehend him. With my mother racing off to murder Thiago, I don't have much time left to help Kari before she's caught up in the chaos. So, when Levi nods at me to follow him, I go willingly.

We scale three fences over to the backyard on the far end of the row before slipping out through the back gate. From there, Jadick and Tripp split off, and while it's tempting to follow them—Jadick being alive solves a hell of a lot more problems than hauling Levi in—I stick with Levi instead.

I refuse to admit, even to myself, that part of me needs to make sure he escapes the danger I've unwittingly put him in with the Indigo Hills mafia pack.

No one else is allowed to hurt my mate except for me.

And they damn sure aren't allowed to kill him.

Considering we ran all the way here, I fully expect to do the same for however long it takes to get wherever Levi has decided to take me. So, I'm surprised when he leads us to the back of the apartment complex and unlocks a creepy white van.

"Get in."

"Seriously? A kidnapper van?"

"It blends," he says simply then climbs in behind the wheel.

I slide into the passenger seat, wrinkling my nose because the inside reeks of him. Pine and spice. It's the best smell in the whole world as far as my wolf is concerned. I hate it.

"Have you been living out of this thing?" I ask, glancing in the back where a futon couch has been folded into a bed.

My stomach does a weird sort of somersault at the idea of Levi in that bed. Or me and Levi in that bed.

"Off and on," he says distractedly.

I face forward again as Levi hits the gas and hops the curb, bypassing the main entrance in favor of a service road behind us.

He's simultaneously watching the road in front of us and the mirrors showing our rearview.

Right. Danger. Not a good time to think about sex. Unfortunately, where Levi's concerned, I'm never *not* thinking about sex.

I roll my window down, hoping the fresh air will clear my head.

Levi gives me a look but says nothing. I have a feeling he can sense my arousal anyway. Stupid mate bond.

We ride in silence, both of us checking for some sign of a tail.

After several miles, it's clear we're not being followed. Satisfied, Levi loops us onto the highway and heads east.

The silence stretches, and inside me sits too many questions to even name. Finally, my brain can't contain them all, and I spill one.

"Are we going to talk about the fact that you've been hiding Jadick Clemons all this time while Crigger gets murdered and his pack goes to shit?"

Levi glances over at me then back at the road. "Are we going to talk about the fact that you brought the Indigo Hills Mafia to the doorstep of my safe house, ruining in one hour what I took six months to create?"

Touché, asshole.

Wait.

"Six months? Are you saying you and Jadick planned his disappearance? That he wasn't kidnapped or held against his will?"

Levi doesn't answer, and my temper spikes.

"You're telling me he's willingly sitting by while Thiago locks Kari in a cell and steals the alpha title out from under him?"

"I'm not telling you anything, actually."

"Fine. You know what, I don't want whatever explanation you might give. I'm sick of wading through your lies."

"*My* lies? You're the one meeting secretly with the mafia and then leading them to my doorstep. Wanting me dead is one thing. Selling me out to Franco Giovanni himself is another."

My jaw drops. Indignation is a bitter taste in my mouth. "I would never… But of course, you think everything is about you."

"What the hell else am I supposed to think? You come looking for me, and the next thing I know, you've led an army of wolves to the very place Jadick is hiding out. Maybe you're not running from Thiago. Maybe you're working with him."

I can't breathe against the rage that boils inside me.

The fucking nerve…

I look wildly around for some outlet, some weapon, some way to react to the insane accusations he's just lobbed at me. But in a moving vehicle, there isn't much to choose from.

Only one thing, in fact.

I unbuckle my seat belt and reach for the door handle, shoving the door open to reveal the highway pavement racing by underneath us at eighty miles per hour.

"What the hell!" Levi yells and swerves, the momentum slamming my door shut again before I can hurl myself out.

Admittedly, it was a reckless plan to begin with.

But when Levi manages to foil it, I only get angrier.

He swerves again, this time onto the shoulder, and then brakes hard enough to throw me forward against the dash. Unbuckled, I grunt as I'm tossed clear of my seat and flattened like a pancake against the glove box.

Levi climbs out of the driver's seat and hauls me up, dragging me to the back and tossing me onto the futon.

When I manage to roll and look up, his gaze is wilder than I've ever seen as he stares down at me.

"Are you insane?" he demands.

"I mean, yeah, probably. Kind of."

My answer seems to make worse whatever mental break I've just caused him to have. He leans down, nostrils flaring.

"I will not let you die, Mac, so stop fucking trying."

"The only thing I was trying to do was get away from you," I snap.

He doesn't answer.

"Oh, so you're the only one allowed to leave in this relationship?"

"What relationship?" he growls.

And the stab of hurt I feel at his words makes me lash out.

"I hate you," I spit.

He growls, grabbing my wrists and pinning them over my head. He's close now, his body pressing down against mine. "You can hate me all you want, Mac. But you will stop trying to get yourself killed, or you'll suffer the consequences."

It takes me a minute to respond, mostly because I'm too busy trying not to arch my hips into his. My nipples are a lost cause. They're already hard enough to cut glass, and I have a feeling he knows it.

Rather than continue to fight, I stop struggling and let my body relax. If it's a fight he wants, then surrender's going to really piss him off. Turning my head, I refuse to meet his eyes as I say quietly, "There's nothing you can do to me you haven't already done."

Levi's reaction isn't the victory I expect, though.

Instead of the insult I've braced for, he lets me go and turns around, balling his hands into fists and letting out a roar that comes from deep in his gut. A roar he's purposefully chosen not to aim at me. More like, he's aiming it at himself.

It jars me more than any retort I expected.

He seems tortured. And that doesn't make sense, not according to the uncaring asshole label I've given him. His emotional outburst makes me feel bad for him, and that's not an emotion I'm comfortable feeling.

I sit up and attempt a joke. A bad one. "We can go again, and this time you can jump from the moving vehicle."

He turns to me, not a shred of amusement on his pained face. He sits down beside me on the lumpy mattress.

"Mac, I know I've hurt you. Deeply. But you have to know that it hurts me too. If you can't trust me, trust your wolf. Trust our connection. I know you can feel the truth in that. What I did to you... it kills me. But it was the only way."

I don't pretend to understand his logic, but I'm done trying to argue it. At least for today.

"I didn't betray you," I say instead. "The mafia guys

were there for me. It had nothing to do with you. And I'm sorry I got you tangled up in my problem."

"Why are they looking for you? What were you doing with Franco?"

I sigh. "My mom knows him. She asked him about the guy who hired the tracker to kill me."

His eyes darken. "Did she get a name?"

"Thiago."

Levi curses. His hands fist again, and I wait while he works to get control of himself. I can't understand why he's so angry about the idea of someone else trying to hurt me, but every time I ask, his answer gets more cryptic, so I leave it alone.

"What are you going to do?" he asks.

"My mom wants to go after Thiago directly."

"Don't you?" he asks.

"I want to save Kari. She's what matters to me."

"You think your mom's method will endanger Kari."

"I do."

"And the mafia?" he asks finally.

"She asked them to babysit me while she 'handles things.' I may have run off before they could lock me up."

He snickers. "They underestimated your stubbornness."

I decide to let that be a compliment. "Anyway, it had nothing to do with you or Jadick. Thanks for helping me get away from them, though."

I look away before he can see my true intentions for coming with him. But Levi's not an idiot, unfortunately for me.

"I'm not going back, Mac."

I let my desperation leak into my eyes as I look up at him. "Not even for Kari?"

"Kari's not safer with me dead," he says. "And we both know that's exactly what will happen if you turn me over to Thiago. I'd wager he'll kill you too when he's done with me."

"None of that would happen if Jadick goes with us," I say.

But Levi shakes his head. "Jadick's more at risk than either of us. Why do you think he went underground in the first place?"

"I get it. Thiago wants to clear out the competition and place himself on a throne of his own making. But if we all work together—"

"I won't ask Jadick to give himself up or put himself at risk for me."

"Kari's his sister. At least, give him the option to decide for himself."

He doesn't answer, and I bite back a slew of curses all aimed at him. There's something else going on, something he's not sharing. Otherwise, none of this makes sense.

"I'm asking for your help," I say, my words sharp.

He arches a brow. "Since when does Mac Quinn need anyone's help?"

I blow out a breath.

"You're not some damsel in distress," he adds. "And I know you too well for you to make me think you are."

"I'm not a monster either," I say, accusation dripping from my words. "Kari's life matters. Even with whatever secret plans you're cooking up, you can't just ignore her in all this. She's innocent."

He hesitates, and I wonder if he's actually thinking all this over or just pretending to.

"If I don't agree, you'll just keep hunting me, won't you?"

I smile sweetly. "Never give up on your dreams. You taught me that."

He could have punched me in the face, and I would have been less shocked than the response he gives me now.

He closes the distance, his mouth covering mine, and every nerve in my body ignites. His kiss is hungry. Like he's starving and I'm the last meal on Earth. His hands grab me, taking, claiming—like he already knows I'm his. And dammit if I don't kiss him back like he's right.

When his tongue brushes mine, I sink into the abyss where all my deepest wants are stored, every one of them named Levi Wild. There's no sense of logic or even time. Only Levi's mouth and hands—and the fact that we aren't naked yet.

A sob breaks loose from my throat, mortifying me the second I hear it. I break the kiss, chest heaving, eyes watering—and I don't know who I hate more. Him or what he's done to me. I can't even enjoy the thing I've spent three years dreaming of.

Levi's ruined me for everyone—even himself.

"I can't..." I say, my voice cracking. "Not like this. Not when... we're still on opposite sides."

Not when you still don't want me in the way that matters.

Instead of backing off, he leans in. His hand cups the back of my neck, and he presses his forehead to mine so I'm forced to shut my eyes or meet his so closely I can read his thoughts.

"Mac, I'm so sorry for all this. And for what's to come. I will never—"

"What's to come?"

I wrench away, staring at him warily. My fingers tingle where they touched his bared throat a moment ago. Every inch of me is still hot, but my brain is struggling to warn me through the fog of my own lust—and it's screaming now.

At the look in his eyes. At the way he shifts closer. Again.

Like he's trying awfully hard to distract me.

"There are things in motion." His fingers stroke my hair. "So much of this began long before you walked into that warehouse. If I could go back and change it—"

"You'd what?"

His eyes are steady on me. Too steady.

Too full of secrets.

Another sob builds. Because whatever this is, it isn't a reconciliation.

The back door of the van is torn open at the same moment the sliding door slams ajar. Both openings reveal men in ski masks. Their scents hit me—a dozen wolves, none of them Black Moon pack.

I jump to my feet. My adrenaline spikes, and my instincts scream at me to do whatever it takes to get away. The logical side of me knows it's already too late.

The thug at the back door reaches for me. I pull my leg back and slam my heel into his nose. He cries out, stumbling back. Hands shove at me from behind, and I careen forward. Giving in to the momentum, I jump out of the van, determined to get free of this corner they've backed us into. But another attacker takes his place, and instead of landing on the ground, I'm plucked out of the air by a vise-like grip. Unfamiliar arms come around me, locking against my torso, bruising my ribs.

I scream, twisting my body in a corkscrew motion in an attempt to wriggle loose. But these guys are professionals. Another one grabs my ankles, neutralizing that particular threat.

When I twist again, I catch sight of Levi exiting the truck, and my heart literally stops beating for long enough that I think I might actually be dead.

If I am, this is Hell.

Because he's not fighting, and he's not being attacked.

In fact, he hops out of the van with an expression that might have shattered my heart had he not done that very thing to it already.

Levi doesn't look at me. That, more than anything, confirms my fears.

"You're late," Levi tells them.

"You missed the rendezvous point by three miles," one of the men snaps. He's the one I kicked in the nose, and I'm rewarded now by the sight of blood pouring from his face and dripping off his chin. "You might have mentioned she'd put up a fight."

"If you'd been on time, she wouldn't have," Levi says.

I stop struggling. The shock of awareness literally paralyzes me.

It's not the fact that he's just out-maneuvered me that's breaking me down. It's the realization that those stolen moments on the futon were all part of his plan to distract me from this.

He set me up.

"Load her up," Levi says, and the two men holding me like a sack of potatoes begin carrying me toward another van parked behind ours.

This one's newer, sleeker. Black with tinted windows. It looks professional like his team. They wear matching dark uniforms, and every one of them moves unlike any thugs-for-hire I've ever encountered.

Something tells me if they get me in that van, it's all over.

I start fighting again, redoubling my efforts. I probably look insane with the crazy-ass way I'm corkscrewing around, but it's the only way I know to break their grip.

It doesn't work.

They get me to the van and toss me in like garbage.

A hand reaches for me, and I catch it with my teeth, biting until I taste blood. The man barks out a curse, and I let him go, spitting his blood on the van's scratchy carpet.

"She's fucking rabid, boss," one of the goons complains.

"Tie her up," Levi says in a voice devoid of any emotion.

It takes three of them to hold me down while one zip ties my wrists and another my ankles. I curse them all using an old Cajun phrase I picked up from one of my mom's marks. The guy rears back, eyes wide through the ski mask he wears.

"What the hell'd you just say?" he demands warily.

"You'll find out in six months," I say sweetly.

He pulls his hand back like he's going to hit me. Before he can, someone else reaches over and presses tape across my mouth.

Assholes, I scream with my eyes.

"That's better," the guy with the tape grunts, eyes narrowed as he backs away.

When they're done, they secure me to a metal rack mounted to the van's interior. Then they slam the door shut.

Outside, I can still hear their muffled voices.

"What is the damned point of all this?" one of the men asks. "If she's this big of a threat, we shouldn't bring her back."

"She's a liability if left alone," Levi says.

"Then fucking kill her, and be done with it." Pretty sure that's the guy with the busted nose. Asshole.

Rather than answering him with words, there's a grunt and then a thud.

Everyone else goes silent for a long moment.

"Get him up and in the other van," Levi says. "Burnett, you take him and your team. Gregario, you're with me. You have your orders. Follow them. And don't question me again."

There's a chorus of "yes, sirs" and then boots on gravel as everyone moves away. Up front, the van doors open, and Levi and another masked asshole get in. The masked asshole drives. Levi doesn't bother to look back at me as we pull onto the road and head for wherever the fuck they're taking me.

I don't know what Levi's up to, but it's clear he isn't who I thought he was.

Not even close.

Levi's the monster here. And I'm officially the thing I've spent my entire life trying to avoid: I'm the damsel in distress.

CHAPTER
ELEVEN

I wake up tied to a chair in a dark room that smells like Levi, and I decide right away that, no matter how much they torture me, the scent will be the worst part of this entire experience.

Pine and spice fill my nostrils, stronger with every inhale.

It's Levi—and he's everywhere.

For a wild moment, I let myself wonder if they aren't piping it in through a vent somewhere as part of some psychological torture method.

The air is damp, and beneath the scent of my scorned mate is the unmistakable musk of raw earth. I'm underground. Or close to it.

No windows.

And the zip ties around my wrists and ankles have been refastened even tighter than before.

At least, they removed the duct tape.

The fact that I slept through it being ripped off

worries me more than anything else. Drugs. Somewhere along the way, I've obviously been dosed. The last thing I remember is being tossed into the back of a van and then—nothing. I search within and am relieved to find my wolf still here. They haven't muted her, which gives me a shred of hope.

A hope that dulls with every new thought.

My mother has gone to kill Thiago. If she succeeds, Kari might die too. And I'm stuck in this underground room, forgotten, while the world burns down around me.

No one knows where I am. Not my mother. Not Tripp. And the list of people who might care, much less rescue me, starts and ends with those two people.

Levi claimed not to want to see me hurt, but clearly that's only because he was saving the job for himself.

My hope deflates like a popped balloon.

I'm so fucking screwed.

I HAVE no idea how long I sit in the darkness, only that it's long enough to make friends with the shadows. When the door opens, I'm not relieved, though. Especially when I see that it's Levi himself framed in the dimly lit opening. The sight of him jolts me—a thousand points of pain that prick all the way to my soul. Or what's left of it. After rejecting me, I thought his betrayal couldn't cut any deeper. I was wrong.

"You're awake." His voice is carefully controlled.

Mine, not so much. "Fuck. You."

He ignores me and turns to someone behind him. "Bring it in."

Another figure enters. One of his security team. Using the light coming in from the room beyond, I recognize his scent from their snatch-and-grab back on the highway. Not the one whose nose I broke, but there's still time.

The guy wheels a small cart into the room and parks it near the wall, still just out of my reach. If my arms weren't bound, that is. As it is, there's no way I can reach either of them, no matter how close they stand. I know. I've tried. And I have the bloodied wrists to prove it.

The guard leaves without a word.

Levi remains.

The door shuts, sealing us both into complete darkness.

A second later, a light clicks on, and I look over in time to see a small switch on the wall near the cart. Then I'm forced to look away, blinking furiously until my eyes adjust to the sudden brightness.

Levi grabs a foldable chair from near the door and opens it.

He sits, facing me several feet away from my own chair.

His eyes are steady on mine. Assessing.

"Whatever you're going to do to me, just fucking do it," I snap.

"What do you think I'm going to do?"

"Besides kidnap me and tie me up? I don't know. Torture. Kill. Whatever you want."

At the last part, something in his eyes flares. A hunger

that sends heat curling low in my belly. I bite my lip. Maybe "whatever he wants" is a little suggestive, but if his goal is torture, taking me while I'm unable to touch him in return would definitely top that list.

As soon as I have the thought, I curse myself and shove it away again. Now is not the time to want him. Now is the time to hate him. Or better yet, kick his ass and get myself the fuck out of his presence.

He blinks, and that hunger is gone.

"I don't want to do any of this, Mac. But you left me no choice."

"Excuse me? Are we victim-blaming now? How in the hell is any of this my fault?"

"You hunted me," he says as if that somehow negates him taking me prisoner.

"You framed me for murder."

Anguish flashes. Maybe even regret. Then, like the hunger, it's gone.

"You're in over your head," he says quietly. "If I hadn't brought you here, you would have gotten us both killed."

"Brought me here?" I scoff. "You mean abducted me. Say the words, asshole."

His expression tightens. "If I untie you, will you run?"

"Of course not." I snort, and he relaxes. "I'll kick your ass, kill you, then I'll run, dragging your dead body along behind me to deliver to Thiago."

He shakes his head. "You still think he'll let Kari go if you bring me in."

He doesn't say it like a question.

More like I'm the idiot if I say yes.

Seething, I refuse to answer at all.

"He's using you, Mac. All he cares about is power. He has a little taste of it now. And he knows he has to eliminate the rest of his family to keep it."

"You'll say anything to save your own ass. You've already made it clear you don't care about Kari. Or me."

The tic in his jaw lets me know I've pushed him too far. He stands with enough force to send the chair toppling behind him. Then he closes the distance, grabbing the back of my chair and leaning down so that we're eye to eye.

"You have no idea who or what I care about. I've tried to tell you, but it's like you don't hear me. What the hell do I have to do to convince you?"

It's like my eyeballs detach from my brain. I drop my gaze to his mouth—just for an instant, but it's more than enough. Levi lets out a growl, and I gasp as his mouth crashes against my own.

My arms strain against the bindings. All I want is to get closer. Logically, I know I should use this opportunity to knee him in the dick, but the only thing I want to touch his cock with right now is my hand or my mouth. I arch into him, pressing my breasts against his chest. Scraping my nipples across the fabric of his shirt.

The friction is delicious. But I want more.

His tongue sweeps into my mouth, plundering.

Levi is taking exactly what he wants, and I can't bring myself to resist—because it's what I want too.

My teeth snag his bottom lip, biting down softly, and he groans.

I whimper, desperate for whatever he'll give me, and his body stiffens.

Instead of deepening the kiss, he pulls back. His chest heaves with labored breaths. The look in his eyes is pure, primal hunger.

I look back at him, uncaring that I've let my guard all the way down. He already has my heart at his beck and call; why not take my body too?

Whatever he sees in my eyes, it's not enough though.

He inches back a little more and exhales heavily.

"Focus on this moment, right here," he whispers, desperation replacing desire. "If you don't believe my words, believe this," he adds, his gaze dropping to my lips then flicking up again to search my glazed eyes. "I will protect you until the day I die, even if it means protecting you from yourself."

My temper stirs.

Desire cools.

This asshole just kissed me to prove a point.

Fine, two can play at that game.

I go with Plan B, driving my knee up and into his groin.

It doesn't quite pack the force I'm capable of, thanks to the bindings trapping my ankles, but it's enough. He doubles over but, unfortunately, recovers quickly. When he straightens, his glare is unyielding.

"If you don't believe my words, believe this," I say, throwing his words back into his face. "I hate you so much more than you seem to hate yourself."

His nostrils flare. "You're stubborn as fucking hell, you know that?"

"And you're a monster."

"You know nothing about what I am. Not anymore."

"You're right. Because you don't tell me shit. You run around with missing alpha-heirs and play ninja all day while everyone else pays the price. What else am I supposed to think?"

When he starts to answer, I cut him off. "You can't kiss your way out of an explanation," I add. "I'm not a man. I can think and have an orgasm all at the same time."

The faintest hint of a smile quirks his lips. "I'll keep that in mind. Though it might be difficult to achieve the latter without the use of your hands—or mine."

Before I can think of something snappy to say, he stalks out.

It's not long before I realize Levi's torture hasn't ended simply because he left the room. In the silence, I'm forced to acknowledge the presence of the food cart he left behind. The scents coming from it are making it impossible to forget how empty my stomach is. That plate of mafia spaghetti is only a memory, and whatever's hiding underneath the tray cover promises to make me forget it altogether.

But Levi doesn't return.

I get impatient. Then I get hangry.

Using my weight against the chair, I sort of hop my way over to the cart. If there are cameras on me, whoever's watching doesn't seem to mind if I help myself.

Fine.

I don't need Levi anyway.

Using my teeth, I pick up the tin cover and let it fall onto the hard floor. It crashes loudly, but still, no one interrupts. I stare down at the plate of lasagna and then let loose with a string of curses—every single one of them a creative alternative to Levi's given name.

Of course, he left me with no fork, no hands, and the only food I can't easily eat without them.

My stomach rumbles, and I seriously debate face planting into the thick pasta, manners be damned.

From the other side of the door, I hear voices. They don't belong to Levi, which means they must be his security team. My wolf hearing picks up just enough to concern me.

"...contain her."

"Levi tried. Clearly, she's not going to cooperate."

"She's a threat to the whole community."

"Drugging her is the only solution."

I look down at the lasagna with a new concern.

Fuck this.

I refuse to go easily, no matter how much of a monster Levi is to me.

Lifting my bound feet, I pull them in and then kick them both out, sending the tray careening backward. It topples over, crashing hard. The dishes break, and the echo of the destruction shatters the silence of my cell.

The door opens, and three guards race into the room.

They stop and take in the fallen cart and broken dishes. Then they each narrow their eyes on me.

"Rude," one of them says, which throws me off only because it's so much more civilized than the response I expected from them.

"Minnie spent a lot of time on that lasagna," says another.

Like it's an accusation.

Like I'm the bad guy here.

"I'm sorry. Where are my manners?" I say lightly then narrow my eyes as I add, "I must have left them behind when you abducted me from the side of the road."

One of the men growls. "You don't want to eat," he says. "Fine."

Instead of coming to kick my ass, he motions to his friends, and they all three walk out again. The door shuts. The lock clicks. And I'm once again alone.

This time with drug-laced lasagna all over the floor. Still, it's better than having it inside me.

I tell myself I won. Or this round at least. But the longer I sit alone in this room, the less I believe it. My hands and feet have long since gone numb yet somehow still ache. Other than that and the fact that I have to pee so badly I might not make it to a bathroom, the only torture happening now is self-inflicted. Over and over, I replay every moment since the one where Levi left me in that warehouse with a dead alpha.

The fact is that I never actually saw him commit that crime. And if I'd been a little less hung up on how hot he is and what a sucker I apparently am for rejection and abandonment, I might have gotten out of there in time too.

Instead, Thiago found me—and used me.

He never cared about justice for Crigger. He cares only for holding onto the power he finally has. Kari's the real victim in all this. Not me.

And I can either keep finding reasons to pick a fight with Levi. Or I can find a way to free her. But first, I have to free myself.

CHAPTER
TWELVE

I drift off, pulled under by exhaustion despite the discomfort of my position. No one returns. Not with food or even water. At first, it feels like a mind game. To show me who's boss. To make me compliant. But then I begin to wonder if they've forgotten about me altogether. Time feels unmeasurable in the dark silence. But I suspect at least a day goes by. Maybe two. My wolf begins to push back at being confined so long, but I don't shift. To do so would use the last of my strength, and I can't be sure the bindings on my wrists and ankles would actually break. They haven't yet despite my attempts. If they don't give during my shift, my legs will break, and that will be that.

Finally, the door opens, and Levi walks in.

Despite my exhaustion, my body reacts. A magnet being pulled to its opposite pole. Even dehydrated, starving, and numb, I can't help wanting him. It's science, not sentiment.

Or that's what I tell myself.

Words feel heavy. The idea of trading barbs is an energy I can't afford at this point. So I remain silent as he strides toward me.

Bracing for whatever abuse he wants to fling at me this time, I am in no way prepared for when he kneels, looks right into my eyes, and says, "I'm sorry."

What?

He produces a knife, and I flinch. He stops, gesturing to the ties that are now embedded against my wrists where they've cut through layers of skin. He brings the knife up and uses it to slice through my bindings. First, my wrists, then my ankles.

I'm too shocked at his apology and suddenly being freed to even use that freedom to fight him. Besides, my limbs are jelly, my circulation nonexistent. The moment I put weight on my feet and attempt to stand, my knees buckle, and I topple forward.

"Whoa." Levi catches me, his strong arms pushing me upright again. "Go slow," he says.

I stare at him in confusion, very aware of where his hands are still gripping my arms—and how nice it feels.

"I went through this in training. I remember how long it took to get proper feeling back into my legs."

"Huh?"

"You look confused," he says uncertainly. "I just meant... I know how you feel because of the training exercises I've done with the team..."

That's not why I'm confused. But I don't bother to contradict him.

Instead, I use the brain power I have left to confirm the suspicions that have been nagging me for days.

"Where are we?" I ask.

He hesitates. "In the mountains."

Something tells me this place matters.

I try a different tactic.

"You're in charge here."

"Yes. No. Sort of." He ducks his head, and I can't quite reconcile a humble Levi with the asshole who locked me up and basically tortured me. "Whoa." He catches me again and waits while I re-steady myself. It's slow going, and Levi seems more and more upset with my condition.

"Didn't they feed you?"

My gaze flicks to where I remember kicking over the lasagna. It's gone, the space clear of any evidence a food cart had ever been there at all.

Levi waits for an answer. I look up at him through the tangled hair in my eyes, too confused and dizzy to be upset. Playing games isn't even an option right now.

"No."

"Come on," he says, gripping my waist and hauling me to my feet.

Our closeness jumbles my thoughts again. We're hip-to-hip, which isn't exactly the most sexual of positions, but all I can think about is his hands gripping my hips, his body fitted against my own.

We take one step together, and I see stars.

Levi catches me even before I realize I've begun to collapse.

My head swims. Lack of sleep, lack of food—lack of a

lot of things—makes it hard to think clearly. Maybe he was on to something leaving me alone so long.

In this moment, I'm too beaten to deny that he's won this round.

"I'm so fucking sorry for leaving you here this long. It shouldn't have happened, but there was an emergency I had to deal with, and I left—" He breaks off, calling out for one of his guys. "Burnett. Get in here."

A redheaded male in dark blue military fatigues appears in the doorway.

"Get her some water," Levi instructs him. "And something to eat. Now."

"Sure."

The guy disappears, spurred on by Levi's urgent tone.

He's not one of the trio from the lasagna incident, which gives me hope he'll actually do as he's asked.

"Come on." Levi grips me tighter and begins moving me slowly toward the door.

I don't resist. I don't even think I could if I wanted to. It's not just the physical aspect, either. His kindness, the apology, it's too weird. Like I've entered some alternative universe that only exists inside this room.

We make it out the door and into the adjoining room, this one larger. It no longer smells like dirt. Instead, the scent of pine and spice slams into me. It makes my eyes water, and I chalk it up to nearly dying of hunger and thirst. But this smell, it makes me thirsty in a different way.

I notice a bed in the corner. It's nothing more than a

mattress on the floor. And it's literally the only piece of furniture in the room. Beside it, a short stack of clothes is folded neatly on a concrete floor.

Levi turns me away from the mattress and helps me across the room. He stops outside another door, this one leading into a small bathroom.

"I'll be right out here if you need help," he says.

"I think I'll manage."

I push the door shut behind me and hurriedly do my business. It's not a big deal in the grand scheme, but I'm pretty sure it's the best pee of my life. When I'm done, I survey myself in the mirror. Tangled, dirty blonde hair falls over my shoulders, framing a face I almost don't recognize. Dark circles ring my eyes, and my cheeks bear traces of the scratches from my fighting frenzy when they brought me in. But it's the hollow look I wear that makes me shudder at my own reflection.

I look like a shell of the badass, capable girl who set out on this journey. I look beaten.

Averting my gaze, I try to remind myself who I'm here for.

Kari.

Not a single soul on this planet is fighting for her besides me. I have to stay focused. And that means I can't afford to kick Levi's dick into his stomach. Not yet.

When I open the door again, Levi's waiting.

"Here." He shoves a bottle of water at me.

The seal hasn't been cracked yet, so I take it and twist it open, drinking until I can't breathe and nearly choke on it. The liquid is sweet relief to my parched throat, but I pace myself. It'll do me no good to throw it up again.

Levi's security guy returns. Burnett. He holds out a protein bar. "Sorry, kitchen's closed, this is all I can find."

Levi frowns and starts to object but, I snatch it away. "It's perfect."

And still sealed.

I peel the wrapper back and break off a huge bite.

"Why wasn't she fed?" Levi demands.

"Grey was in charge of it," Burnett says with a shrug.

"Tell him to meet me after his shift," Levi snaps.

"You got it."

Burnett walks out, and we're left alone again.

I stand there and scarf down the entire bar then finish off the water without breaking our silence. By the time I'm done, I am mildly convinced I can walk unassisted. My feet and legs are tingling with the feeling of blood returning. My hands work well enough.

Still, Levi actually looks ... sorry. Or something close to it.

"How long have I been in there?" I ask.

He hesitates. "Two days, give or take."

Two days.

Damn.

No wonder I'm coming apart at the seams. My mother trained me for all manner of fighting—offense, defense, and everything in between. But I've never trained for a scenario like this one. Capture. Torture. And the fact that Levi's my captor... I have no idea what to do or say next.

But he's watching me like it's my move.

"What's the matter with you?" I ask.

"What do you mean?"

"I don't know. You're being...weird. Apologizing, bringing me water, food."

He chuckles darkly. "You mean nice?"

"You kidnapped me and kept me in a locked room for two days without food or water. Let's not get carried away."

He sighs. "Look, I had to do something drastic to—"

"Don't say you're keeping me safe."

"All right." He gestures to the door Burnett left through, and, I suspect, whatever lies beyond. "I'm also protecting the people in this community."

I glance around what looks like a fallout shelter. "What community?"

He hesitates, clearly debating whether he can trust me. I don't give him any false hope, but finally, he nods anyway. "Come on. I want to show you something."

He leads me down a series of short hallways. We don't pass anyone else, but I can hear voices somewhere nearby. The building is squat with low ceilings and very few windows. "Compound" feels like a fitting word. It has a military feel with function prioritized over comfort.

But it's not cold or even dangerous.

Not like Thiago's house.

Maybe I've been left alone too long because I should feel endangered by a place that held me against my will, but more than anything, I just want to understand. What makes this place special enough that Levi would lock me away just to keep it safe?

And why in the hell does he think I'm a threat to it in the first place?

"What's this?" I ask as we pass a hall and I hear music drifting out from an open door.

Children's songs.

"A few of the families that live here have little ones," he says and then tugs me forward.

Children?

Families?

What the hell is this place?

We keep moving, and Levi quietly points out a few more areas. "Rec room," he says, and I glimpse a ping pong table and video game console through the glass doors. "Gym, laundry, showers."

Community, the men had called it.

I see that now.

Up ahead, the hum of voices grows steadily louder until Levi stops me in front of a set of wide double doors. A security guard stands beside them.

"Sir," he says when he sees me. "Is this wise?"

"She's fine, Grey. No thanks to you."

"Sir?"

"We'll talk about it later," Levi says. "Move."

With a glare aimed at me, the guy pulls the door open, letting us pass.

As soon as I walk in, I stop and sweep the large room with wide eyes. My senses tell me there are at least forty, maybe fifty people seated around the long rectangular tables. A few are still finishing whatever dinner remains on their tray, but most have finished and are chatting with their neighbors.

The smell of food draws my attention, and I see a kitchen running along the right side of the room. True to the guard's word, it's closed now. The lights are dark up front near the serving stations.

A cafeteria.

And a crowd.

Every one of them is a wolf shifter.

Most are dressed in the same fatigues as Burnett.

Out of all the things Levi could have been hiding from me, an entire army of shifters under his command was the last thing I would have guessed.

Finally, I turn to look at where he's waiting at my elbow. He's watching me with an eagerness that looks disturbingly like hope. I don't understand it. Or him. Or any of this.

"Who are these people?" I ask.

He nods at the crowd. "This is my pack."

"Your...."

I can't even say the word. It's too busy punching me in the gut. The word "pack" suggests a bond closer than family. Closer than, in this case, a mate. And it stings even though it shouldn't.

"Your pack," I manage through gritted teeth.

He nods. "Mac, meet the Jades."

Another sucker-punch.

The Jades.

Not *a* Jade.

There is no girl he's running off to be with instead of

me. I should feel relieved at the misplaced jealousy I felt back at that hotel. But I don't.

Somehow, I think this is worse.

Instead of one girl, he's traded me for a whole new family. He's truly moved on with his life, and the evidence is staring back at me, reflected in every face in this room.

CHAPTER THIRTEEN

My eyes widen as I look out over the sea of faces. They've begun to notice me now too. Slowly and then all at once, conversation begins to quiet until the entire room goes silent and they're all staring back at me with some sort of expectation I already know I can't meet. Or don't want to.

"Everyone, this is Mac Quinn," Levi says. "Mac, this is everyone."

No one speaks.

"They're staring," I say to Levi.

"They heard you were hunting me," he says.

I whip my gaze to his. "You told your entire pack?"

He shrugs. "Our bond runs pretty deep. I couldn't keep it from them. Not when there was danger."

Their bond.

The words are a knife twisting slowly.

I stare back at every one of their curious faces, resentment simmering in my blood. It's not their fault Levi used them to hurt me. But they're going to feel the consequences. I couldn't reject him three years ago, but I can reject his people now.

"What are you looking at?" I demand of a woman closest to where I stand.

At my harsh words, she ducks her head and turns around.

Levi stiffens, but he doesn't comment.

Slowly, conversation resumes around us, but I can feel their edginess. Like they expect me to attack Levi right here in front of them.

I arch a brow at him. "You must think I'm dangerous if it means warning your pack about me—and locking me up to keep them safe."

But instead of hurling an insult or a threat, he grins, and my knees nearly buckle at the sight of it. After only a slight wobble on my part—and honestly, it's a miracle I don't crumple—Levi's grin turns to a smirk.

"Mac, you have no idea what kind of danger you put me in."

Something about the way he says the words makes me wonder if we're still talking about the fact that I want to trap his ass and then turn him over to our enemy.

"This must be the infamous Mac."

I look over as a woman I've never seen before strides up with two male guards close at her heels. One of them is the redhead from earlier, Burnett. I recognize the other male from the van-grab. The one who managed to wrestle me into submission. My expression tightens at the sight of him, but I force myself to focus on the woman who obviously outranks the two men, judging by their formation behind her. Her gray-blonde hair is cropped short and combed back to reveal a pair of steel-blue eyes that don't waver from my own. Her uniform is less "military" and more "manager" with black pants and a matching jacket. But her posture and stance don't fool me.

This chick can fight.

And she dares anyone to make her prove it.

"And you are?" I say, not in the mood for bull shit power plays.

"Frankie Dyer."

She doesn't offer any other greeting than her name.

Fine by me.

I don't bother to reply.

"Frankie," Levi prompts because she's clearly come with a message. When the woman hesitates, he adds, "You can speak freely here."

She doesn't look particularly agreeable to that idea, but she does it anyway. "The teams are on their way in now." Her gaze flicks to me. "Where should I have them debrief?"

"We'll meet them in the hangar," he says.

She looks even less thrilled about that, but she doesn't argue. When she walks off, her two shadows follow.

"She seems friendly," I joke.

"You want her trust, earn it."

His response is clipped.

I glare at him. "I don't want anyone's trust. I want to save my friend."

He hesitates as if putting aside whatever he really

wanted to say. "Fair enough. First, don't you want to see what's in the hangar?"

I roll my eyes. "Sure. Hopefully, it's an armored vehicle I can use to run you over with and then make my escape."

"Without me?"

"Of course not. You're in the trunk in this scenario."

"Naturally."

He holds my stare, and for some reason, I have to make an effort not to smile. Asshole.

"Come on," he says, and this time when he leads me through the halls, I can at least feel my feet again.

"So, what team was she talking about?" I ask. He glances at me knowingly. "What? Just trying to make conversation."

"No, you're trying to gather intel while also counting doors and mapping exits." He points at a door before I can argue and says, "Let me help. That one leads to the roof."

"I wasn't—"

"And that one leads to the basement."

"You're an ass—"

"Oh, don't forget the janitor's closet."

I shove hard, slamming him into the closet door hard enough for his head to make a loud *thump*. He grunts at the impact, and I use the element of surprise to land a punch in his gut.

"I'm done playing house," I hiss. "You're coming with me. To end this."

He doubles over, but his recovery is faster than I anticipated.

Before I can bring him fully down, he's straightening

and shoving me off him. He grabs my shoulders, twisting me toward the wall, and slamming my shoulders against it.

I struggle, but his grip is too tight to shake.

His eyes are like granite as he stares down at me. His chest rises and falls with labored breaths.

"Last warning, Mac. Try that again and I'll lock you up for a lot longer than two days."

I bite back the urge to scream at him. He's beaten me more times than I want to admit. But worse than the injury to my pride is the threat it poses to my friend.

"My mother is out there," I say, my voice cracking as my control finally slips. I am near tears, but I can't bring myself to care. There's no pride left in me where Levi's concerned. He stripped that away from me a long time ago. "If she kills Thiago, he's given orders to do the same to Kari. If that happens, it will be on you."

"Don't worry about your mother," he says. His voice is rough, clearly unmoved by my emotional display. Asshole. "And stop being rude to the people here. They've done nothing to you."

He steps back, releasing his hold on me, and I nearly crumple. My sense of urgency wars with the cold reality that I will never accomplish my task in time to save Kari. My mother has never failed a mission yet, and I don't expect her to start now.

Resigned, I hang my head.

Levi motions for me to walk with him again, and after another ragged breath, I obey.

He begins pointing out doors again as if the past few

minutes' interruption never even happened. If he's bothered that I've just tried attacking him on his home turf, he doesn't show it.

"Conference rooms," he says, gesturing to a closed door. "And this."

He pushes through and I follow.

On the other side, I find myself in a large open area with high ceilings and enough space to park at least a dozen vehicles comfortably. The left side of the hangar already holds four vehicles. A Range Rover, a couple of older sedans, and a motorcycle, but the right side is empty.

At the far end, the large bay door is wide open. From here, I have a straight, unhindered shot to the outside world. I can also hear the distinct hum of several vehicles approaching, which means I have a feeling I wouldn't get very far if I tried to run.

Then again, why would I do that when my target is standing six inches to my left?

"The hangar," I guess.

He nods toward the opening as the first of a convoy pulls in. "And the teams," he adds.

We stand back while they all park, six vehicles in total. Four are dark SUVs like the one Thiago used to banish me from pack lands. The other two are armored trucks similar to what I've seen banks use to transport money.

"So, what, you decided to start your own mafia pack or something?" I ask, trying to understand what the hell is going on here.

Levi shakes his head. "Not quite. Although, the mafia

pack used to be part of a larger pack and then broke off on their own, so in that, we're similar."

I shoot him a look that undoubtedly conveys my confusion. "You started your own pack. You're in charge here... Does that mean you're alpha?"

"Something like that." His smug smile makes me want to punch him in the mouth. "Impressed?"

I roll my eyes, turning away, because, well, yeah.

Becoming an alpha is about a hell of a lot more than just finding people willing to become your pack. You have to fight for it. To bleed for it. Making an alpha takes more than most are capable of giving. To survive the process is a feat in itself. The fact that Levi's done it and lived to tell me about it? Yeah, that's impressive as hell.

But he clearly knows that and just wants to hear me say it.

Like hell.

"What is the point of bringing me here?" I ask. "To show off? You're an alpha. You have a pack. A security detail. Expensive cars. Whatever. You don't need to impress me; you need to outrun me."

He turns to me, something slippery in his gaze now. Like he has a secret. Or lots of them. "I don't want to impress you, Mac. If I did, we wouldn't have left the room where I kept you. In fact, I wouldn't have untied you either."

His words are unexpectedly erotic, and the desire that punches me in the gut steals my breath.

Levi leans in, knowing full well what he's doing to me now.

"You're not impressed by status, Mac. I know what impresses you, remember? Or have you forgotten what it was like to have my hands on you? My mouth?"

"We never..."

He's so close, his mouth brushes mine when he says, "Not yet."

I nearly lean in and give myself over to the promise in his voice. The sharp sound of a car door slamming brings me back to the present moment.

I gasp as Levi sidesteps me and goes to meet whoever is coming this way. Voices sound behind me.

I take another deep breath to steady myself, except the air is full of his scent, so all it does is threaten to choke me with desire. I force myself to turn anyway—to look unaffected by what's between us.

The teams climb out of their cars and shout hellos to one another, to Levi, their alpha. My gaze sweeps past the dozen or so men headed toward where Levi waits. I spot a familiar face among them.

Tripp.

His fatigues are dusty, caked with dirt. And he looks tired as hell. He offers a weak smile when he sees me, but the worry in his dark gaze is too pronounced to ignore.

Beside him is another face I recognize.

Jadick.

He's back, and his swagger is stronger than ever, unfortunately.

He looks directly at me, and in that stare is a complete disregard for anything other than his own agenda. When I don't immediately avert my gaze from his, he cocks his head at me. Curious. Interested. Clearly not used to anything but cowering.

What a jerk.

Behind them, one last car door slams shut, and a lone female figure catches my eye. Her gait is hurried though it's not purpose or concern that has her cutting a quick path through the others and straight toward me.

No, this is anger, pure and cutting.

Vicki Quinn glares at me with all the fire she possesses. Her hair is mussed, and there's dried blood on her cheek, but otherwise, she looks unharmed. I'm shocked to realize I was actually worried about her.

Then I look around for anyone else they've brought.

But Kari isn't here, and for a moment, I can barely breathe around my own fear. Has she done it then? Has my mother killed Thiago? Did Tripp and Jadick help? But if so, why would Jadick come back here? Something else must have happened. But I don't get a chance to ask what before my mother's temper spills over.

"You and I need to talk, young lady," she says to me.

For once, I don't care that she looks madder than a hornet and prepared to aim all that ire at me. I'm too relieved to see her here in one piece. And hopefully, Kari is too.

"Hi, Mom."

I can feel Levi's eyes on my back, but he doesn't interrupt this little reunion. He orchestrated it after all. Instead, he stands a safe distance away, chatting with his men. With Jadick.

"Don't 'hi, Mom' me," she snaps. "You called me in to

your little friends before I could complete the mission. What the hell, Mac?"

Relief hits first. Thiago's alive, and that means Kari is too. Then I frown, glancing at Levi then Tripp, who's standing on my left, far enough out of the line of fire.

"I didn't call you in," I tell her.

"If you didn't, then who did?" she demands.

Silence rings out across the hangar.

My mother's sharp gaze cuts to Tripp.

He looks a little nervous as he says, "Levi ordered your extraction. What was I supposed to do?"

Her eyes widen, and she pushes past me, marching toward Levi. I hurry to catch up, not quite sure where this is headed. My mother never quite warmed up to Levi, and now? I'm pretty sure all sorts of retribution are on the table.

"You ordered my extraction?" she demands. "Before I could put an end to that little shitbrick?"

"It was a hasty move, Vicki. One we can't afford at this stage, you know that."

"Mom, listen, I—"

"Hasty? Are you kidding me?" She jerks her thumb at me as she goes off. "You brought *her* here and are letting her walk around like she's one of us, and you're questioning *my* decisions?"

I flinch as if she slapped me.

Us?

Levi doesn't answer, but his face reddens. I can't tell if he's embarrassed or angry, but at this point, it doesn't even matter. I can barely form words around the brick pressing down on my chest.

"You know about this place?" I ask.

My voice is small. I hate it, but I can't help it any more than I can help change what they've clearly already done behind my back.

"Of course I know," my mother scoffs like it should be obvious.

I take one look at their faces—Levi, Tripp, even Jadick—and in this moment, it *is* obvious. They've all been working from a master playbook and never bothered to give me a copy. Or even tell me, we were playing a game.

I look away from my mother. From Tripp. And I don't even attempt to look at Levi. Every face I see is someone else who has or will betray me.

It's disgusting.

I back away.

"Hey. Wait."

When Tripp reaches for me, I jerk away from him.

"Mac, don't be dramatic," my mother says, and it's the last thing I hear before I turn and run.

CHAPTER
FOURTEEN

Outside the hangar doors, the land is barren and empty. Far off, the horizon is dotted with purple mountains, but here, there is a valley's worth of dead grass and dirt for what looks like miles. Overhead, clouds mute the daylight, washing the sky in hazy gray.

I have no idea where I am—or where I'm going—but it's not enough of a reason to stop. Not after the betrayal of everyone I know waiting behind me. My wolf rises to the surface, carrying me faster over the hardened ground.

I push, pumping my arms, lengthening my strides.

My bones begin to creak, and I'm only a breath away from shifting when I sense someone coming up on my flank. My first instinct is to turn and fight. Even if it's Levi. Hell, especially if it's him. But then his scent hits me, and I'm too surprised to do anything but maintain my pace. Out of everyone who might have followed and attempted to coax me back, he is the last one I expected.

He matches me easily, his even strides putting us shoulder to shoulder. Instead of trying to stop me, he continues to run alongside me.

I look over.

Jadick looks back.

I debate shifting, trying to run for it, but what just happened back there has stolen my drive. Or maybe it's our "kidnapped" alpha heir running quietly at my hip.

Ugh.

I stop, chest heaving, lungs burning, and face him.

He stops too, but I see none of the frustration in his gaze that I know is in mine. Only curiosity. As if he's wondering what I'll do next. Although, I get the sense he doesn't care either way.

"You're a coward," I say, glaring at him.

His brows lift. "I'm not the one running away from my problems. Literally."

"Aren't you?" I shoot back. "You're out here, hiding, while your entire pack thinks you've been kidnapped—or worse."

"Touché, little Quinn."

"Don't call me that."

"But it's your name."

"My name is Mac."

"Fair enough. Why are you angry, Mac?"

"Because they lied."

"Ah. Right." He looks like he understands, but then he blinks, and the confusion returns. "And why do you care what Levi does?"

"I don't."

His lips twitch. Asshole. "Of course."

Something about his smug, know-it-all expression forces an explanation out that I don't even want to verbalize. Not to him. "My mother has controlled my entire life. Making me into some version of her while still making all of my choices for me. When she decided killing your brother suited her, there was no changing her mind. She actually tried handing me to the mafia for safekeeping." I put the word into air quotes. "And now I find out she's been in on Levi's little secret life this entire time? It's infuriating. If he doesn't want me in his life, he doesn't need her either."

"You care an awful lot about who he has in his life, considering you want to let my brother kill him."

His words grate on me, and I bare my teeth. "You know nothing about what I want."

He holds up his hands in surrender. "I'm just trying to understand. To help."

"If you want to help, go home, and knock your brother off his throne."

"Actually, I plan to do just that." His eyes glint, and I recognize his manipulation—but I'm too invested in what he's just said to care.

"You do?"

"Yes, and I don't mean to sound callous about your very real predicament, Mac—" He emphasizes the use of my actual name this time—"But I'm not out here to chat about your broken heart."

I bite back the urge to deny his accusation.

"Then why are you here?"

"Because I could use your help."

"You want my help," I repeat uncertainly.

Not because I don't want to offer it. But I can't imagine how I might contribute to his plans. Without Levi or Crigger's murderer, I have nothing.

"May I voice an observation?"

I shrug. "Sure."

"You are a fighter, mostly because it's what you were trained for. And what you know. But more than that, you are a strategist. You see the bigger picture, and you assess. I'd wager you're constantly assessing, in fact. Risks, rewards, exit points."

"You seem to think highly of me, considering you barely know me."

"Knowing you and understanding you are two very different concepts, don't you agree?"

The way he speaks… like he sees me in a way no one else has—it throws me off balance.

"If you think I'm such a strategist, what's my strategy for leaving now?" I ask, trying to regain my footing.

"I don't think you're leaving at all."

"No?"

"If I hadn't come after you, Levi would have. Or Tripp. And even if they hadn't, it wouldn't have mattered anyway. Eventually, your emotions would clear, and you'd realize the only way forward is to go back."

I hate that he's right.

"I don't care what you think of me," I say. "What I care about is saving Kari. I promised, and that's not something I take lightly."

"I don't intend to stop you. Your loyalty is the precise quality that makes you so valuable."

"So you say." I hesitate, biting my lip while I do the exact thing he probably expects right now: strategizing. In the end, I give him what he wants, though. Because it can only help me get what I want too.

"What do you need me for?"

His grin is a slow, victorious thing. Like I've just fallen into the center of his web. "Come on, Mac. Walk with me."

He reaches over and slings an arm around my shoulders as if we've just become besties. Then he angles me back toward the hangar and starts walking.

I don't resist when he leads me back toward Levi's little camp. Mostly because I'm curious about Jadick's plan, but there's a part of me that needs to see this place for what it really is.

To understand.

Levi gave up everything, his home, his life, his mate—for this. A fresh start with people he clearly cared more about than he ever pretended to care for me. I need to know why. Even though I'm pretty sure whatever I learn is going to make me hate him—and myself—even more than I already do.

"Thiago has always been blinded by his own ego," Jadick says as we walk.

I snort. "Tell me something I don't know."

"All right. Did you know he had my mate killed?"

Sympathy tugs at me. "I heard. I'm so sorry."

"My brother has always seen me as his biggest threat.

And he's spent his life punishing me for it. Unfortunately, he didn't limit his ire to just me."

"Kari," I say.

"Yes, and our parents."

"You think he killed your father."

"Don't you?"

"I have my suspicions," I say. "But what about your mother?"

"My mother's death is unexplained to this day. A rogue tracker found her in the woods, yet no contract existed for a payout of her death."

"Trackers don't work for free," I say darkly, thinking of the one Thiago sent after me.

"No," he said, "They don't. But it would have taken someone with great power to cover their tracks. My father's alpha power couldn't penetrate the tracker's mind during interrogation."

"I never even knew he tried."

"My family worked hard to keep these details secret. If word got out there was this much bloodshed among us, we'd become a target for others as well."

"I get it, but… if alpha power couldn't penetrate the interrogation, what does that mean? Thiago's just not that powerful," I say, shaking my head. "Sure, he has motive but not necessarily means."

"You're as smart as they say," he says.

"Why do you sound so surprised?"

He laughs, which seems a bit out of place given the topic of our conversation. But then, he's spent his life under the weight of Thiago's hatred. Maybe he's learned to live with it. "Not surprised. Delighted."

He winks, and I look away, uncomfortable. But Jadick goes on, clearly unbothered by my reaction.

"I am skeptical myself," he says. "Maybe my brother is more powerful than I gave him credit for."

"Or maybe he's working with someone," I say.

He gives me an appreciative look as if I've somehow impressed him again. "Maybe," he agrees.

"Is that why you ran?"

My words have a bit less bite this time around, but the accusation is still there. I can't help it.

"I left because he tried to have me killed. And I realized I was no longer sure I could trust the people around me not to help him. Thiago's not a kind person, but he's convincing when he wants to be."

They have that in common then.

"He'll promise you whatever you want to hear if it gets him what he wants," he adds.

I think of Kari. Of the deal I struck to bring Levi back to take her place.

And I remember Levi's warning to me. That Thiago never intends to let her go. Not while he considers her a threat to his position.

"Okay," I say, "All of this history is interesting, but it still doesn't explain what you plan to do to stop him or to rescue Kari. Not to mention why you need me."

We're nearly back inside the hangar now. Close enough that I can see Levi still waiting for us where I left him. My mother and the others are gone along with Tripp. I don't know whether to be pissed about that or grateful that he's given me space. He and I will have our own sort of showdown later. But for now, I keep my eyes on Levi as Jadick goes on.

"The Jades were created to stand in the way of stolen power," he says.

"An army to overthrow Thiago," I realize, looking around at the faces of the men and women working to unload vehicles or transport supplies. At his words, I see them all in a new light.

Maybe I don't resent them after all. Maybe we all want the same things.

"Levi thinks we need bigger numbers, but I disagree," he says as we make our way to where Levi waits for us.

"What do you think?" I ask.

Levi scowls as we come to a stop in front of him. Whatever he feels about my swift exit, it's not showing on his face now. Instead, he looks solely focused on Jadick and whatever master strategy he's about to lay out.

"Thiago's ego has always been his downfall," Jadick goes on. "He'll show his hand soon, and when he does, we'll prey on that weakness. Use it as leverage to draw him out. He'll sabotage himself. He always does."

"Uh, he's managed to bypass his own father and you as the heir. And he's current pack alpha," I say. "I'd say that looks less like self-sabotage and more like success."

Levi looks like he wants to agree.

Jadick shakes his head, not bothered by my doubt. "Thiago's always been too rash. Too quick to act. He doesn't think things through. Take Levi for example. Or me. Coming for us only made us fight back that much harder."

"I don't follow."

"Look around you. Thiago thinks he chased us off. Meanwhile, we've been building a haven and collecting everyone he's ever pissed off." He winks. "Trust me, taking Thiago down will be easy."

"It would be a hell of a lot easier if we had the numbers," Levi mutters darkly.

"You worry too much, brother. Do you not have faith in me?" Jadick asks, and I wonder how he can't see the irony of accusing Thiago of a big ego.

"What do you think it'll take if not an army?" I ask him.

He ticks them off one by one. "Cunning. Wit. Patience. And you."

"Me?"

"Thiago expects you to return with a murderer, doesn't he?" Jadick asks.

"Yes."

"You are the only one of us who can walk right through the front door without resistance. When you do, bull's eye."

"You want me to draw him out and then what? You'll shoot him from a rooftop or something?"

"You have a better idea?" he asks.

"No, but... the rules of the pack say you can't become alpha that way. You have to challenge him. Fight—"

"Times are changing, Mac. Aren't they, Levi?" He looks sharply from Levi and back to me. "You all want change so badly. I'm willing to do whatever it takes to get that change."

Levi says nothing.

"So, you want me to do your dirty work," I say.

"We all must play a role."

"And saving Kari," I say. "Who's role is that?"

"This is ridiculous," Levi says. "She's not an assassin for hire. I told you, this is what the Jades are for."

Jadick waves him off and smiles at me. "Think about it, Mac. You'd be a valuable addition to our cause." Before I can answer, he turns to Levi and claps him on the back. "I'm going to turn in, brother. See you both in the morning."

He strides away, disappearing through the door leading back into the compound.

Then he's gone. And I'm alone with the guy I came here to kidnap, who actually, it turned out, kidnapped me instead.

Levi looks at me with an expression I can't read. "You came back."

"Jadick's convincing that way."

Something angry flashes in his eyes.

"Kitchen's open again," he says. "For the crew just arriving."

I think about going back into that crowded cafeteria, facing those people who looked at me like they want to kill me.

"I'm good," I say. "Where's Tripp?"

"Probably still eating."

"And the others?"

"Everyone else has gone to bed."

Bed.

For some reason, I think of that mattress on the floor, and my face heats.

"I had a room made up for you," he adds, and I wonder if he's read my thoughts somehow.

"I'm not staying."

He cocks his head at me. "Aren't you?" When I don't answer, he adds, "What about Jadick's plan?"

"Jadick said a lot of words without actually telling me anything."

His brows lift. "You seemed into it."

"Jealous?"

"Should I be? You stuck around and listened to him in a way you never have with me."

"He didn't publicly reject me and then spend years working with my own mother behind my back to accomplish the very thing you promised we'd do together."

His eyes narrowed. "Is that how you see this?"

"How else should I see it?"

His voice rose. I'd finally shaken his control. Good. "You could try seeing me as something other than the villain of your fucking story."

"When you start *being* something else, I'll *see* something else."

His eyes narrow, and he grabs my arm, walking me backward toward the wall. Unlike earlier, I realize I have a choice. He's not forcing me. But I don't fight it. Or him.

My shoulders thud against the wall, and Levi crowds

me, filling my personal space until I'm practically breathing him.

"I think about you every day," he whispers, his voice strained. "My wolf still wants you just the same as it did before. No." He closes his eyes slowly, inhaling me so deliberately it feels erotic, despite the fact that we aren't doing anything but standing here. "He wants you even more."

His voice is ragged. Raw. He's barely holding it together.

I can smell his lust just like I know he can smell mine.

"I did all of this for you," he says.

"Bull shit," I whisper, and his narrowed eyes register hurt at my response. I'm too shocked at seeing it there—at knowing I caused it in the first place—to continue my argument.

"Every single day since the moment I turned you away has been torture, Mac. Why can't you see that?"

"Because you left me," I say, letting my own broken heart show in my eyes. "You did the one thing you swore you wouldn't, Levi. You rejected me. And you did it publicly. It was the worst day of my life. And I think about you every day too. About that moment. I'll be reliving that nightmare every single day—forever."

"I'm sorry," he says, bending low until our foreheads touch.

He means it.

I can feel the genuine desperation—the pain—radiating from him. His wolf hates this. So does mine. But it doesn't change what he did. Or what we are now, which is nothing.

He angles his face, his mouth inching toward mine.

He's going to kiss me.

And I want to let him, but I know instinctively that if I do, it'll be like forgiving him. He'll think it's okay, that I'm not mad anymore. That he's allowed to destroy me and then come crawling back. Maybe it would have been okay, but I know I won't survive it twice.

It takes everything in me to turn my head.

To push him away.

He stumbles back even though I've used barely any force.

The way he looks at me... it's exactly how I feel about him too.

"Mac," he says, and my name is a plea.

He's begging.

But I can't pretend he didn't break me once. And I'm too damn strong now, thanks to his cruelty, to ever let him do it again.

CHAPTER
FIFTEEN

Despite the late hour, my mother is sitting on top of a table surrounded by half a dozen soldiers when I finally enter the cafeteria. Even from across the room, I can tell she's in the middle of some exaggerated story of one of her more dangerous takedowns. The sad part is she doesn't have to exaggerate. My mom's a badass. She's the best bounty hunter I've ever met. She's just not great at feelings.

When I get close, she smiles at me but doesn't bother to pause her story. I'm not surprised, but that doesn't stop me from being pissed.

I stop short of shoving a few of Levi's guys out of my way. Instead, I cross my arms and glare at the woman in the spotlight.

"Can I talk to you?"

She stops her story and offers me a tight smile. "Sure, honey." She hops off the table, and the guys part ranks to give her space to pass.

A couple of them groan at the interruption. She winks back at them. "I'll finish later, boys. I always do."

A couple of them laugh.

My jaw drops, and nausea rolls in my stomach. "Mom, if you could wait until I'm gone to hit on the younger ones, that would be great."

"Relax, they're all at least old enough to buy me alcohol."

I grit my teeth. This was a mistake.

"You know what," I begin as we pass into the hallway, but she grabs my shoulder and steers me into the room across the hall.

"Come on, we can talk in here."

She flicks on a light to reveal a small conference room complete with a table and half a dozen rolling chairs. A whiteboard is mounted to the far wall, filled with a bunch of scribbles and acronyms. This is some sort of planning space for them. I eye the board, but none of it makes sense.

The click of the door behind me makes me whirl, and I start in immediately.

"I cannot believe—"

I don't get far before she interrupts me. "Mac, I owe you an apology."

"You do?" I can't help the suspicion. Years of experience.

"Of course. I know it must hurt to find out I've been in contact with Levi when he wouldn't so much as send you a Christmas card."

I stare at her.

This is her idea of an apology?

"The truth is, I stumbled upon his operation purely by chance about eighteen months ago while hunting down a mark. Once I realized what he was doing here, I knew it was smart to hedge my bets and offer what value I could."

"Hedge your bets?"

She shrugs. "I mean, you never know which way these things will go. But now that Crigger's gone, and Jadick's almost ready to make a move, I think they have a real shot."

I huffed. "Unbelievable. And does Levi know you were just playing the field until you felt his team had a real shot? Or does he actually think you're loyal?"

"Does it matter?"

"Of course it matters."

She shakes her head. "Oh, to be young again and have such conviction."

Her wistful smile only pisses me off further. "Oh to be old and not give a shit about anyone but yourself."

Her smile falls. It's not anger that flashes back at me but something more like resolve. "All right. You want to talk about giving a shit, let's start with Levi. He built this place from the ground up. Mostly as a haven against Thiago, who wouldn't stop hunting him when he uncovered Levi's plan to accept you as his mate."

"Wait, what?"

Thiago knew about our plans?

"Oh, you didn't know that part? Well, let me go on. Thiago's been screwing with anyone he deems a threat for as long as he could walk and talk. And honestly, the womb was probably no picnic either, but Delores isn't around to verify—which should speak volumes. Anyway, the point is that the entire family has one goal, and that's to survive one another." She pauses, finally noticing my stricken expression. "Are you listening?"

"Levi really intended to accept me?"

She rolls her eyes. "Why am I not surprised you're stuck on that?"

"Does Thiago have something to do with why Levi rejected me?"

"You'll have to ask him."

Tripp's words from the hotel come back to me. He *did it to protect you.* My thoughts race with the possibilities of what that might mean, but my mother steps closer, crowding me enough that she has my full attention.

"I need you to hear me on this, Mac. You can run off to your mate once I'm done, but this is important."

"What is it?"

"Hear me when I say that family has the same one-track mind."

"What is that supposed to mean?"

She speaks so low I can barely hear her. "Jadick is the same as his brother. He wants to be alpha by any means necessary. That puts him on our side right now, but don't think for a second it can't swing in the other direction. The wind always changes, darling. Don't forget that."

"You don't trust him?"

"Not with my daughter."

"We finally agree on something," I say in a low voice.

Instead of irritation at my tone, I get a, "Good girl."

She heads for the door.

"Mom."

She pauses, her hand on the knob as she looks back at me.

"Thank you," I tell her almost begrudgingly.

"I didn't spare Thiago for you," she reminds me.

"I know that."

She studies me carefully. "Will you be here in the morning?"

I look away. "Maybe."

"You still planning on trying to drag Levi back to Blackstone?" she asks wryly, and I realize she knows I've been beaten by a mark—for the first time ever.

"Depends on whether he leaves me a choice."

She looks torn. "I would have preferred to keep you out of this, but what's done is done. Don't forget what I said."

"I won't."

"And get some sleep. Whatever they're planning, it might not involve letting me kill Thiago, but you'll need all your wits for it, I'm sure."

She doesn't wait for my response before letting herself out.

Her warning isn't concerning.

I have zero doubt Jadick intends to use me. There's no mistaking the sweetness in his voice. The flirty smile he shoots me when I ask the right question. But I'm using him too.

I intend to survive his family. And I intend to save Kari from them too.

The only real sucker punch my mother gave me has to do with the guy I just rejected back in the hangar for no other reason than wanting to hurt him the way he hurt me once.

His words from earlier ring in my head. *"You could try seeing me as something other than the villain of your fucking story."*

What if my mother is right? What if he's never been the villain at all?

CHAPTER SIXTEEN

Movement in the doorway startles me out of my spiraling thoughts.

"Tripp," I say, exhaling at the sight of him.

"Sorry, didn't mean to scare you." He runs a hand through his hair, expression tight. "Everything okay?"

"Yeah, fine."

The pause between us is awkwardly full. I want to say something—*anything*—that will bring back the friendship we once had. But that friendship didn't include secrets, and now we're so full of them that I can barely see him at all through all the words left unspoken between us.

"My mom's in the cafeteria, holding court," I say. "If you're looking for her."

"Actually, I was looking for you."

"Oh."

"Well," he says after a moment, looking everywhere

but at me. "I'm sure you're tired. I can show you where you'll sleep."

I start to refuse, to tell him what I told Levi—I'm not staying.

But in the end, I give in and let him lead me back through the maze of beige-colored hallways. The turns are slightly familiar now, and I work on committing them to memory, once and for all. My mother is right. Whatever Jadick is planning, I can't afford to let my guard down.

The halls are empty of everyone but us. The only other people we pass are two guards stationed at the hangar door, which lets me know it's the only way out. They don't make eye contact with me as we pass.

Even walking right beside my former friend, I sense a distance between us that hurts my heart.

Finally, Tripp shows me into a small room.

"I made some room in the top drawer if you need to store anything," he says, gesturing to the dresser.

"This is your room?" I ask, surprised.

He shrugs. "There aren't any singles left empty so I figured... I'll sleep in a hammock in the hangar for now."

"Thanks," I tell him, unsure what else to say.

It's a nice gesture. But I'm not sure how to be "nice" to Tripp after everything.

"What was this place?" I ask, glancing around at the nondescript walls. "Before, I mean."

"A human army base," he says. "Training camp or something. One of the Jades had a connection and knew they'd shut it down, so we took it over. So far, no one's been the wiser."

"How long have you lived here?"

He eyes me warily. "If I tell you, are you going to punch me?"

His words sting, mostly because it's a valid question. But I can't bring myself to answer it seriously. Somehow, I think that would make it worse.

"I make no guarantees either way." I cock my head, showing I'm teasing. "You worried you can't fend me off, Thompson?"

He snorts. "Please, Quinn. You're lucky I've gone easy on you all these years."

"Oh, yeah, I'm super grateful for that."

Our smiles fade, and too soon, the awkwardness is back.

"There's a granola bar and water for you." Tripp nods at the dresser and then turns to leave. For some reason, the pre-wrapped food melts my heart. It's clear he understands my distrust of these people, and whether or not he agrees with it, he's willing to meet me halfway.

"Tripp," I call.

He stops, eyeing me with a gaze still full of secrets.

My shoulders sag.

"Good night," I say.

"Good night."

Sleep is slow to come.

I lie awake, listening to the silence and trying to ignore the isolation of this place. Or maybe that's just the awareness of betrayal.

If Levi really did intend to accept me, he's had three years to tell me the truth. Three years of no contact and then three days' worth of nonstop lies. I don't know how to pretend either of those things away.

I can't excuse it.

All I can do is hope this all leads back to Kari—and try not to get my heart broken all over again before I get there.

THE NEXT MORNING, I venture warily out of my room, only to find the hall notably empty of guards. Either they decided I wasn't going to run after all, or they didn't care either way.

The cafeteria is packed for breakfast. Despite the crowd, there isn't a single familiar or friendly face among them. No Levi. No Tripp. Not even Jadick or my mother is around.

One particularly harsh face steps into view, blocking my path.

Grey.

The one who made sure I didn't eat or drink for two days.

My hands ball into fists. "What the hell do you want?"

"You shouldn't be allowed to roam alone."

"Are you going to stop me?"

He starts to answer, but a short barked order cuts him off.

"Grey. Back off."

We both look over to see Frankie cutting a path through the onlookers.

Her hair is still damp from a shower, and her uniform

is freshly pressed. Her entire vibe is "don't fuck with me," which I appreciate, though I would have rather dealt with the asshole myself.

"Don't you have somewhere to be?" she demands of him, standing toe to toe with the asshole despite the six extra inches of height he has on her.

"She should have an escort," he snaps at her.

"Consider me it," she says in a voice that dares him to argue.

Grey looks me over, his lip curled in a snarl that makes it clear what he thinks of me. Then he turns on his heel and leaves.

"Don't pay him any attention," Frankie tells me.

The rest of the cafeteria slowly goes back to their own business.

I exhale, not sure whether to be relieved or disappointed I didn't get to kick the guy's ass.

"He tried to starve me to death," I say, "so, yeah, he's going to have my attention—at least until I can repay the favor."

Her brows lift. "I see. Does Levi know?"

"Yeah."

"And Grey's still breathing?" Frankie asks wryly.

I frown. "I'm not sure Levi cares quite that much."

She snorts, but her amusement dies at the sight of my expression. "Give it 'til end of day," she says. "If Grey's still walking around like he owns the place, you have my full permission and support to lay him out."

"Noted," I say.

She pats my arm. "See you around, Mac."

"Bye."

She disappears toward the food line, leaving me alone to navigate. Ignoring the glares and whispers, I manage to snag a plate of pancakes and a water before retreating back into the hall. My stomach grumbles at the sound of it and I realize how long it's been since I had a real meal.

The idea of returning to my tiny room is too unappealing. Instead, I duck back into the conference room from last night. While I eat, I try to decipher what the coding on the whiteboard means.

Behind me, someone knocks lightly on the open door.

I look up to see Levi standing there, and a hundred emotions wash over me. Even after hours apart, the look he gives me takes me right back to where we left off in the hangar last night. His eyes swirl with need, and I nearly give in and throw myself into his arms right here. Then a second figure enters behind him, shoving him aside so he can pass.

"Move, bro," Tripp grunts good-naturedly. He stops short when he sees me, though. "Oh. Hey."

I wrench my gaze from Levi and look at Tripp. "Hi."

The awkwardness reaches a new level with the three of us in the same room again.

"I was looking for my mother," I say lamely.

"She left early this morning," Levi says.

"What?"

"She didn't tell you?"

I sigh. "Of course not. Why would she?"

He hesitates. "I'm sure she was just busy with the details of whoever she's hunting down this time..."

"Don't defend her," I snap.

He falls silent.

In that silence, I only feel worse.

"We were just—" Tripp begins.

"Listen," I say at the same time, but then Jadick arrives, and I clamp down on whatever sentimental thing I'd been about to indulge in.

Pushing to my feet, I prepare to make myself scarce. Whatever they're here for, it clearly has nothing to do with me.

"Hey," Jadick says with a flirty smile. "Glad you're here. I was just going to look for you."

"You were?" I ask warily.

"We'd like to invite you to stay for a status update on the Thiago situation," he says. "Care to join us?"

My eyes widen, but Jadick doesn't react to my surprise. I look from him to Levi, waiting. But even if Levi's in charge out there, with the men, in here, it's clearly Jadick at the helm.

"Okay," I say, still off-balance.

But I'm not going to turn down information.

Levi rounds the table, and Tripp follows. They both take a seat. Jadick motions for me to take one too. I sit across from Levi. Jadick sits beside me.

I scoot away as much as possible without making it obvious.

"What's this about?" I ask.

"We'd like to make sure everything's on the table." Jadick smiles. "Pun intended."

Tripp rolls his eyes. "Terrible," he mutters.

"That sounds good," I say, doing my best to focus on the information he's offering to divulge. "We can start with who made the call to extract my mother and why."

"I made that call," Levi says.

I'm not surprised. They'd said as much yesterday. But his admission means I'm forced to meet his gaze. There, I find way too many layers of emotions to unravel. Instead, I shift my eyes to a spot on the wall just over his head.

"Why bother?" I ask. "Not that I'm not grateful, but she would have eliminated your enemy for you. We all know she's capable."

"Because of this." He sets his phone on the table between us and hits play on a voice mail.

Thiago's voice fills the room.

"Levi, brother, I hope you're well."

The smugness in Thiago's voice infuriates me, but I force myself to keep quiet and listen.

"You may have heard I've struck a deal with your little Reject. Quinn is on the hunt for a killer, and I've taken my sister as leverage until she brings me one. The people want justice for my father's murder, and I intend to get it for them. In the meantime, please warn the little Quinn that should any harm come to me, I've left instructions that Kari should meet that same fate."

There's a blood-curdling scream that abruptly cuts off.

Thiago chuckles darkly, but I barely register the sound. My own heart has dropped to my stomach.

I look up at Levi.

He's already watching me.

"Sounds a bit like our previous arrangement, eh?"

Thiago adds, clearly amused with himself. "In case there's any confusion, that deal also still stands."

Click.

The call ends.

My heart pounds.

"What deal?" I ask.

Levi doesn't answer.

"What deal?" I repeat, louder now.

"You didn't tell her." Jadick's tone is surprised.

I spare a glance for Tripp, who keeps his eyes on the table.

Every one of them knows something I don't.

"I will tear this compound apart, and then I'll run back to Thiago and sell all of you out if you don't tell me about this deal right the fuck now," I growl.

"Everyone out," Levi says.

His voice is barely above a whisper, but it's deadly.

Tripp and Jadick exchange a glance and then get up from their chairs.

"Don't be too hard on him, Mac," Jadick says.

Levi looks ready to punch him.

"Not now," Levi says in a tight voice.

I catch a twinkle of satisfaction in Jadick's eye, but then he ducks his head and walks out behind Tripp.

When we're alone, I push out of my chair and stand against the far wall. It's stupid, really. There's nowhere I can go Levi can't reach me. His hooks are in too deep.

He looks up at me, and the connection between us pulls taut.

"Thiago came to me three years ago," he says, voice

devoid of emotion. "He knew what you and I planned to do... accepting one another as mates. Proclaiming ourselves as Romantics. He threatened you. He said— He said he'd kill you if I didn't reject you."

"You're serious?"

"I would never lie about this, Mac."

I don't know what to think. Everything I know about Levi—about what he did—paints him as an asshole. A villain.

"And you believed his threat?" I can't help but scoff.

"You think I'd risk it?" he asks, eyes blazing with intensity. Before I can answer, he adds, "I knew he'd do it because he did it to Jadick first."

"Right. Lacey." I almost forgot. "But Jadick rejected her," I say. "And Thiago still killed her."

"Exactly. Imagine what he'd do to you if we mated."

His words are laced with pain, and I know he's done exactly that: imagined all the ways Thiago would have hurt me. Still, I can't simply accept this explanation. After three years of hating him, I can't just turn it off.

"You could have told me—"

"I cannot lose you," he roars.

He's out of his chair in the space of a blink. Rounding the table, pressing rough hands to my cheeks. "I love you, Mac. I have loved you since the moment I first laid eyes on you in seventh grade when you punched Pete Bolling in the nuts for stealing Tripp's lunch money."

"He was a bully."

He smiles. Or tries to.

"You are more than my mate, Mac. You're my whole

fucking heart. I couldn't possibly have done anything other than what I did. Telling you would have risked you. Defying Thiago would have risked you. Coming back for you would have risked you. Don't you get it by now? I will never, ever do anything that could hurt you."

"Except that you did."

His brows dip. Confusion mars his desperation.

I pull free of his grasp, and he lets me. His hands drop to his sides. He's never looked more lost. I've never felt so angry.

I fist my hands, pacing in front of the whiteboard now.

If Levi's not the enemy, who is? Because I have to find somewhere to put all this rage. I don't even have to ask. I already know. Thiago.

All that pain. My life, my happiness, my mate—stolen from me.

For what?

A family feud?

Power?

A fucking title?

"Jadick's going to challenge him," Levi says, obviously reading where my thoughts have taken me. "It's the only real way to end this."

"Jadick's right about Thiago," I say. "He has no honor. He won't fight fair. Not even in a challenge."

"Then we'll all fight," he says.

"Thiago already has Crigger's entire army," I say. "They've pledged their loyalty. They'll fight."

"I have an army too."

"That's why you created the Jades? To fight for Jadick?"

The name, it fits.

But he shakes his head. "I didn't create the Jades. I may have brought us together to this place, but I didn't create them. To be a Jade means you're tired of the way things are in Blackstone."

"Wait. They're all from our pack?"

He nods. "Some left years ago. Others joined us more recently. But we're all done with Crigger's rules. These people want change, Mac. Same as we do. And they're willing to fight for it."

"They're jaded," I realize, and he offers a rueful smile.

"Too on the nose?"

"Not any worse than Romantics and Rejects, I guess."

"I just wanted a place where I belong," he says, and I wonder if he's thinking of his parents. "Where maybe someday we could belong together."

His smile fades as he waits for me to respond.

He created this place, brought these people here, to fight back. Not for Jadick. For me.

My heart swells.

Hope.

It's almost too much to feel. I can't remember the last time I let it in. And the urge to shove it out again is so practiced I nearly do it. But then I stop myself.

Trembling, I close the distance he's put between us.

He's completely still as I come to a stop before him. Like he doesn't want to spook me. I don't blame him. But I also don't want to run. Not anymore.

"You never wanted to reject me?" I whisper.

I am terrified of his answer—of having this hope crushed.

"No, Mac. I never wanted to reject you."

My eyes fill with hot tears. I blink them back. His expression softens, and he reaches up to cup my cheek again. Slowly, he leans down, and my breath catches.

I don't move.

I don't even breathe.

If anything ruins this—

But nothing does.

His kiss is soft. Achingly gentle and more like a memory come to life. I melt against him, my hands reaching for his shirt, his skin, his hair. Whatever I can find. I need to feel him against my fingertips.

When I wrap my arms around his neck, he growls. It's a primal sound that wakes my beast, and I make a sound of my own—pure lust and need—and then the kiss is no longer soft or sweet. He grabs my hips, yanking me against him. Unsatisfied, he lifts me so that our bodies meet and meld in all the right places.

I cling to him, desperate and agonizingly hungry for more. His kiss is hot and rough, his tongue plunging into my mouth like a demand. He spins so that I'm pinned against the wall, and, with one hand cupping my ass to hold me steady, he slips the other hand beneath my shirt.

His fingers dip inside my bra, closing around my already hardened nipple and expertly flicking it until I'm squeezing my thighs in a silent plea for more.

"Mac," he groans, pulling his mouth from mine so that he can trail kisses down my throat.

My fingers are tangled in his hair.

My control is long gone. No memory I possess compares to the reality of Levi touching my body.

His hand releases my breast and dives lower, rubbing at my already soaked leggings. For once, I don't stop myself from grinding against him.

"Please," I whimper.

He snarls, mouth finding mine again and swallowing my sounds.

Still, it's not enough. There are too many clothes between us. Too much space. I want him inside me. I want him to consume me. Maybe then, I'll begin where he ends, and no one can ever come between us again.

The door opens.

It's a sound I'm only mildly aware of and honestly too worked up to even care.

But a voice shatters the breathless silence. "Levi."

He goes still against me.

His head whips toward the door.

I see Jadick standing in the opening, looking anything but ashamed at walking in on us like this. If anything, he looks weirdly into it. My face heats, and I lower my legs, sliding down the wall so that I'm standing on my own feet.

"What?" Levi demands, his arm still around me.

"There's been an incident." Jadick looks between us. "You're needed in the hangar."

"Fuck," Levi mutters, and Jadick glances at me one more time before leaving us alone.

I look up at him, unnerved by the afterglow of our little moment. But he stops me from pulling away, and instead of hauling ass for the hangar, he leans in and gives me a lingering kiss.

"What's that for?" I whisper.

"For later," he says and then steps back.

He grabs my hand; a clear message he has no intention of going back to pretending we hate each other. "Come on," he says. "They're waiting for us."

CHAPTER
SEVENTEEN

In the very back of the hangar, a small security contingent forms a loose circle. Grey is one of them, but for once, he doesn't seem to notice me. He's too focused on whatever he's guarding. In the center of the circle, Jadick and Tripp stand over a man on his knees. It takes me until I'm three feet away before I recognize him through all the bruises and dried blood caked across his skin.

"Dirk?" I stare at him in complete shock. The sight of him alive at all is unexpected enough. But how the hell did he get *here*?

"You know this guy?" Tripp asks.

Dirk stares up at me with a bleak expression.

I tear my gaze from his and focus on Tripp, who's clearly waiting, along with Jadick and Levi, for an explanation.

"Not exactly. He was a mark. Crigger hired me to bring him in before..." I don't finish before I'm turning back to

Dirk, eyes narrowed in suspicion. "What the hell are you doing here? And how are you alive?"

"He's here because this is where he lives." Levi's voice is soft but not gentle.

I turn to him, startled. One look at his face, and I realize my knowing Dirk has somehow shattered the trust we'd just rebuilt between us.

"Dirk is a Jade?" I look from Levi to Tripp and finally to Jadick, who doesn't seem quite so disturbed by my involvement with the bloody dude kneeling at his feet.

"Dirk has been working as an informant for us," Jadick explains.

"He went dark a couple of weeks ago," Tripp supplies.

A few possibilities dawn on me, and no matter which one ends up being true, I know I've stepped in some shit that makes me look like a real asshole right about now.

"Look," I say, "Crigger hired me to bring him in. I had no idea what for. I just needed the cash—and to stay on his good side."

"Because you cared so much what that asshole thought of you," Tripp says, and I glare at him.

"I care about staying alive and out of jail. Or have you been hiding behind these walls so long you forgot what it's like to survive in Black Moon?"

He doesn't answer.

None of them do.

But my temper is hot now, so I keep going.

"I brought Dirk in despite the fact that he and three of his friends tried to kill me for it."

A muscle in Levi's jaw twitches at that, so I decide to

leave out the part about Dirk trying to force himself on me.

"You know I'm telling the truth," I say to him, "Because you saw me with him the night you left me in that warehouse to take the fall for Crigger's murder."

Tripp and Jadick look at Levi.

He sighs. "She's telling the truth." He flicks a glance toward Dirk. "I didn't recognize him that night."

"How could you miss that detail?" Tripp demands, but Levi shoots him a look sharp enough to silence him.

"I was distracted," he says simply, and no one argues.

No one looks at me like I'm the traitor anymore either, so I keep my mouth shut. Levi taking my side is too foreign for me to know how to react.

In the silence, I crouch so that I'm eye-level with Dirk. It's clear now that they haven't forced him to his knees out of some attempt to dominate him. He's simply too weak to stand.

"I thought Thiago would have killed you," I say.

"Been moments I kind of wish he had," he admits.

My heart pangs with guilt. Despite what Dirk tried to do to me, I can't help feeling like his injuries are my fault.

"Thiago tortured you," I say, and he doesn't answer.

He doesn't need to.

Levi's hand closes around my arm, and I let him pull me to my feet. Jadick moves into my spot and crouches in front of Dirk.

"You're safe now." Jadick places his hand on Dirk's shoulder. "But we need to know what you gave up, brother."

Dirk's expression crumples as he relives a pain I can't even imagine. "I held out as long as I could," he says gruffly.

"I know you did," Jadick says and nods in encouragement for Dirk to continue.

My heart begins to thud harder as my senses pick up the nerves coming from the others. They're worried. Levi's only ever played it completely cool with me. No matter how bad things were, he's never been worried. So, the fact that he is now puts me on edge in a way that makes my skin crawl.

I focus on Dirk, holding my breath while I wait for his answer.

"I don't know. It's a little fuzzy," he says, voice cracking.

"Try to think," Jadick says a little more forcefully now. His hand squeezes Dirk's shoulder.

Dirk winces. "Okay, fine, I told him about the Jades," he rasped. "I couldn't help it. My body gave out. My control was gone. He drugged me, and I just started talking—"

"Did you give him our location?" Jadick snaps.

His voice is a whip, silencing anything but the answer.

Dirk's broken whisper is a roar in my ears. "Yes."

Levi stiffens. He doesn't look at me. No one does.

"Evacuation protocol?" Tripp says though it's not much of a question.

Jadick stands. He and Levi share a look.

"Do it," Levi says.

"Dammit," Jadick mutters, but he doesn't disagree.

"What about...?" Tripp nods at Dirk.

Jadick uses a two-way radio to call for medical support, and within moments, two Jades in scrubs arrive to help treat Dirk's wounds. I watch, wondering if they can see what I can: Dirk's physical wounds will heal, but judging from the haunted look in his glassy eyes, nothing they do will make him forget what he went through.

He was tortured.

Because of me.

"I have to make the rounds." Levi's voice is an anchor in my sea of chaos, and I force myself to pay attention.

"Rounds?" I ask.

"I need to be sure everyone's following protocol. Can you stay here? Wait for me?"

"I'll stay with her," Tripp says when I don't answer.

Levi hesitates.

"I won't take my eyes off her," Tripp insists. "Go."

Levi squeezes my hand once, and then he's gone, hurrying through the hangar and barking orders to everyone in sight. Jadick is already gone, I realize. And so is Dirk.

Tripp pulls me into a hug.

I let him, startled by the fact that he's shaking.

Not him, I realize.

Me.

I'm in shock.

Freaking out in a way my training usually prevents.

But nothing has prepared me for this. I'm not worried for myself. I can handle whatever happens next. It's all the people inside these walls—their endangered lives—that fill me with a guilt so thick I can barely breathe through it.

Get it the fuck together, Mac.

Tripp finally lets me go, and I hate to admit that his arms around me helped steady me. He studies my face, his hands pressing against my cheeks so I can't escape his perusal.

"Breathe," he orders, which makes me wonder how much of my horror is showing on my face.

"I am," I say, but even I can hear the lie.

"In," he orders, and after a beat, "Out."

I follow his direction. After three deep breaths, I feel a little more like myself. Around us, people rush in every direction. Their energy becomes more urgent with every passing second.

"It's going to be okay," Tripp says, letting me go.

He glances at the vehicles currently being loaded with people. I can already see that there won't be enough room in them for all these bodies. And who knows what sort of threat is headed our way already. If we'll even make it out in time.

"No," I say, "It's not."

"Don't," Tripp warns, eyeing me knowingly.

"I did this."

His gaze hardens into a stony resolve. "No," he says firmly. "That prick Thiago did this. Don't let him get off that easy. He's the one who'll have to pay." He grips my shoulders. "And we *will* make him pay."

I shake loose of his touch, not sure I fully believe that anymore.

"Yeah," I say anyway. "Okay." I straighten. "What can I do?"

"Put her in the truck," Levi says before Tripp can answer.

I look up to see him leading a dozen men through the hangar, every one of them dressed in nothing but shorts.

"I'm not taking a spot in one of the cars," I say.

Levi frowns. I brace myself for an argument.

"Tripp, take them to the perimeter. Organize and start sweeps," Levi says.

"You got it." Tripp gives me a sympathetic look. "Don't do anything stupid," he tells me and then jogs off with the security team.

I turn to Levi. "I'm not going to argue about this."

"Good. Then it's settled."

My eyes narrow. "There isn't enough room as it is. I'm not taking up a spot that should go to someone else."

"The truck is armored," he says. "It's safer for you there."

"And what about all the women and children? Will they be safer?" He scowls. "Where will you be?" I press.

"Running with the others."

"Good. I'll do that."

He looks ready to argue or maybe even toss me over his shoulder and throw me into the closest trunk. I plant my feet, ready to fight him off, because there's no way I'm taking a spot away from a mother or her child.

"Let her run with us."

We both turn to look at Jadick. His hands are full of supplies.

"She's shady as hell," he adds when Levi doesn't answer. "Probably best to keep her where we can see her. Besides, we need her for the plan."

"I already told you that idea is too reckless," Levi begins.

"I'm in," I say quickly.

Jadick beams at me. "Atta girl. Okay, let's get these vehicles on the road. See you at the checkpoint?"

"Fine," Levi mutters, and Jadick strides away.

I try—and fail—to hide my victory.

"Don't look so smug, Mac. If you're running with me, that means I will tackle your ass before I let you do something stupid."

My response is muted by a horrific boom.

Around me, people scream, but I can't hear them through the temporary deafness in my ears.

Dust and rock rain down around us. Instinctively, I put my hands over my head, which isn't really necessary since Levi grabs me and pulls me down to the floor with his body covering mine. We land hard against the stone, and I grunt as Levi's weight settles against me.

A large boulder rips loose from the ceiling and slams into the concrete beside us. I jerk at the sight of it and feel the reverberation of its impact all the way through my bones.

I'm still recovering from it when Levi yanks me to my feet again. His face looms in front of me, eyes wide and urgent.

"Follow me."

His words sound as if they've come from underwater.

But I make them out, barely, thanks to the shape of his lips as he talks.

I nod, and he grabs my hand, pulling me through the hangar.

He shouts orders to the people around us, but I can't hear them.

The vehicles fill quickly as everyone climbs in, and Levi yanks me out of the way as each of them accelerates for the exit. Another explosion rocks the hangar. More stone tears loose from above and beside us.

Twice, I'm nearly crushed but manage to jump clear of the falling debris.

My feet barely keep me upright, thanks to the shaking ground. Beside me, a woman falls. Her cries are cut off as she lands face first in a pile of rubble with a boulder as large as a car on top of her.

I glance behind me and see others also pinned or lying still and bloodied in the broken piles of stone and debris. My chest squeezes, and I falter, wanting desperately to turn back and help. But Levi's expression as he yanks me toward him—toward the exit—makes it clear that's not an option. And deep down, I know it won't do any good. They're gone. And if I try to go back, I'll die with them.

More explosions sound above my head. Boulders fall, and the walls shake with the force of their impact. Every inhale draws another cloud of dust into my lungs, and I choke as I leap over the uneven ground. The hangar is crumbling, falling apart with us still inside it.

If I didn't know what this was, I'd assume an earthquake.

But this is no natural disaster. We're under attack.

Thiago has found us.

Dirk sold us out. And I put him in the exact right place to do it.

The remaining Jades sprint through the hangar opening with us. One by one, they all shift into their wolf, and we pour out of the doorway into the dusty air. In the distance, red taillights are fading as the convoy drives off. Levi steers me toward the trees, and we run with the others, shifting as we go.

My clothes tear away from my body as my limbs lengthen and pop. One second, I'm a human, and the next, my wolf is eating up the ground with her long strides and massive paws.

Behind us, the Jade compound continues to crumble as more explosives detonate topside. I have no idea how many men Thiago has sent to kill us, but I have no doubt that's what will happen if we don't fight our way past them.

We're all being hunted now.

CHAPTER
EIGHTEEN

We make it to the base of the mountains before Thiago's men catch us. In the gorge, at least a dozen men appear and begin to drop from above, repelling off the craggy rocks and blocking our escape. As the first few hit the ground, we fan out. I bare my teeth, muscles bunched and ready as I square off with a man still tethered to his drop cord. He produces a blade and cuts the cord then immediately shifts. Before I can sink my teeth into him, Levi is there, cutting past me to take the man down into the hard dirt.

I growl, mostly out of the need for a fight of my own, and look for another opponent. The wolves who came with us are nearly all engaged in fights of their own. We're closely numbered. Unless reinforcements show up for Thiago's men. A likely scenario, considering the damage they've already done to the compound itself.

We need to win this fight, and we need to do it fast.

Another man drops from above.

I meet him before he has time to complete the shift, my teeth ripping into his shoulder and tearing a chunk away. His blood and tissue coat my mouth, but I spit it back at him before darting in for another bite. This time, I come away with his throat, and his cries of pain die out at the same time he does.

I spin and look for another.

Levi appears, breathless and with a hard gleam in his eye. He nods for me to follow him away from what's left of the fight. Reluctantly, I do.

We haul ass through the gorge, increasing our speed only when the rest of our ranks finish with the enemy behind us and catch up.

I do a quick count as I run.

We've lost two more.

As much as I want another chance for vengeance, I find myself hoping we don't run into any more soldiers. Every life lost is another life I feel responsible for losing.

Thiago wanted this.

He planned for it.

But I gave him the opportunity to make it happen.

At nightfall, we finally stop to rest.

We're deep in the mountains now. My wolf senses are alert for threats, but aside from that first attack in the gorge, we've met no one else. Up here, the air is colder. A crisp scent of pine and dirt. My wolf enjoys it—or she would if we weren't here because Thiago was hell-bent on killing us all.

The others gather around as Levi takes his human

form again. "We'll rest in this system of caves," he tells them. "Start again in the morning."

"Jadick will worry," one of the men says.

Grey.

I've managed to keep my distance from the asshole all day, but now, I want to take a bite out of his jugular. My temper still rages beneath the surface, and I have nowhere to put it. He seems as good a place as any.

"Jadick will worry more if we're reckless," Levi says. "We still have men out there patrolling to make sure we aren't followed. I won't leave them behind."

Grey doesn't argue.

I force myself to relax.

"Burnett, Grey, take first watch," Levi adds. "Wake me to relieve you."

Returning to wolf form, the two men begin climbing for the high ground to take up their positions. The others disburse as well, breaking off into groups of two or three and disappearing into the shallow caves we've found lining this ridge.

Still in wolf form, I wait, watching Levi.

He looks back at me with exhaustion lining his expression. The shadows have gathered, making it hard to see details, but this close, I can't ignore his naked body. Even my wolf finds his human appearance attractive.

It's a weird sensation.

Finally, the silence stretches too long, and I wonder if I've mistaken his interest. When I turn to go, he stops me.

"Will you stay with me?"

I try to think of a reason to refuse him, but in the end, I follow him into the darkness of an unclaimed cave.

Inside, the shadows are thick, the darkness so complete it takes a few minutes for my eyes to adjust.

Levi remains human.

He ducks out again, leaving me alone so long I give in and lie down. My eyelids begin to droop, and by the time he returns, I'm fighting sleep.

I watch with lazy focus as he goes to work building a fire. When the flames are crackling, he approaches me and holds out a patchwork of leaves someone has strung together with vines.

"For you to sleep more comfortably," he explains.

He sets it down in front of me and backs toward the fire again.

I watch him go, wide awake, thanks to his sudden closeness.

"We'll have to hunt for something to eat in the morning," he adds.

My wolf is interested at the prospect, but my human side grimaces. Nothing like taking down a rabbit for brunch.

Levi stares at me from where he's perched on the other side of the fire.

"You can shift back if you want," he says.

But I don't move.

"Seriously, Mac. I know you don't love staying in this form for this long at one time." He hesitates, looking away before adding, "I'll keep you safe tonight."

His words pierce me, and I give in to the need to be

human again.

"I can keep myself safe," I say quietly.

His eyes snap back to mine, and his expression softens. "Hi."

"Hi yourself."

"Are you okay?"

"I'm not injured."

"That's not what I meant."

I bite my lip. Honesty isn't my first instinct, not with Levi. But tonight, I find myself trying it for the first time in years. "I'm sorry," I say quietly.

"For what?" he asks, startled.

"For letting Dirk be taken. For...what happened at the compound."

"That wasn't your fault," he says.

"That's nice of you to say." I shake my head. "But I had a hand in it."

"I saw Dirk with you that night. I'm just as much to blame as you are for his capture and torture." "Besides," he adds, his words almost a challenge. "I would have thought you'd be glad to see the compound go. You weren't exactly welcomed into it with open arms."

"I can still appreciate what it meant to you. That place was your home. The people who were killed were your pack—and now they're gone."

At my words, whatever mask he'd worn before drops away. Raw grief shines in his eyes, and I feel the depth of it like a punch in the gut. I realize too late what a gaping wound my words have uncovered. For all his stoicism and leadership today, he is broken by this.

His expression is bleak as he says, "You would think I'd be used to loss by now, but it doesn't really get easier."

His voice is ragged. He won't look at me.

I find myself blinking back tears.

"Levi..."

Despite everything between us, my heart hurts at the sight of his pain. At knowing I helped cause it.

"I didn't set out to create a new pack, you know. I didn't mean to become an alpha either. It just... I went looking for my parents."

"Is that why you left town?" I ask. "I always thought it was to escape me."

He finally meets my eyes. "It was," he admits. "But only because of Thiago's threats. His blackmail meant I couldn't afford to give in to temptation. And I knew if I stayed..." He sighs. "Well, I think we've already proven we can't keep our hands to ourselves when we're in the same space."

He tries for a smile, but it's more of a wince.

"Did you find them?" I ask, needing to change the subject. To talk about anything except the tension between us. Even now, in this cave, with the threat of an attack hanging over us all, I can't think about anything except the sight of Levi's ripped chest in the firelight.

Thankfully, the rest of him is hidden in shadows, or my self-control would have dried up long before now.

"Your parents," I add when he doesn't answer.

He blinks as if breaking through his own distractions. "No," he says. "I found Grey. And Frankie. And then more and more of them. All of them used to be Black Moon. And all of them wanted their lives back." He smiles. "Then one day, Tripp showed up, and it was all kind of a smooth slide into pack life after that."

"Tripp has a way with people," I say.

"He's sneaky," Levi agrees. "In a good way."

I don't answer. I want to agree, but then I think of how he kept the truth from me. How they all did. Even my mother.

"Where will you all go?" I ask instead.

"Tripp and I have a few possible locations scouted," he says.

"You planned for this."

"We planned for contingencies." Something about his words trips something in me.

"You knew this might happen."

"I'd be an idiot not to consider it. And the possibility became more likely when Jadick joined us. So I had Tripp look into a few places. There's an abandoned shopping mall outside of Wythe. Looks like the city planned to reinvest and revamp but ran out of money, so it's just sitting. We can go there at least until we figure something else out."

I don't respond.

The silence stretches between us with a thousand words left unspoken. I try to accept it. That this night is our last together. That no matter what, in the end, he'll choose the Jades, and I'll be left alone to fulfill my promise to Kari. I try to accept that tomorrow we'll be enemies again.

But just for tonight, I can't help enjoying that what's between us now feels something like friendship.

Tonight, we're on the same side. Just for a little while.

"You could come with us," he says, and I stare back at him, surprised he's said the words aloud. We both know my answer won't be yes.

"I promised Kari," I say simply.

"You need a plan, Mac. Somewhere safe to figure out what's next. Wythe is safe—"

"I won't hide."

"Is that what you think I'm doing?" His words are sharp now. "These people rely on me. Women, children. They have nowhere else to go."

"They chose to leave. That's not on you."

"Every single person here is a victim of Crigger's toxic way of life. Since the moment we became a pack underneath a black moon, we've been doomed to choose between death or a life of misery. We've been enslaved by Crigger's twisted ideas. These people are risking everything to escape that."

"You want to talk about choices, Levi? Give me a break. I didn't even have that. You made my choice for me. And when you left, Kari was there for me. Not you. Not Tripp. Not even my mother. I don't put my life above hers because, without her, I wouldn't be here. So, maybe these people risked everything to escape. But for me, there is no escape. The pack doesn't trap me. My feelings for you do that all on their own. So, fuck escape. I'll risk everything for loyalty. At least, I still have something to fight for."

CHAPTER NINETEEN

I regret my words the minute they're out. I don't deny they're true, but the look on Levi's face as I say them weighs me with guilt. Knowing the truth and speaking it are two different skill sets. He is silent for a long moment; long enough to make me feel like shit. He's already grieving, and I've basically kicked him while he's down.

Finally, he pushes to his feet. "I better relieve the guys for watch," he says, turning away before I can respond. "Get some sleep," he adds.

Then he shifts and slips out of the cave, leaving me alone with the fire and my own hollow regret.

I sleep fitfully, which is pretty normal for me, but between bouts of actual rest, I have nightmares of Levi running off and leaving me to wake up alone on this mountain.

The morning is drizzly and cold, but contrary to my dreams, Levi is still here. The others are already assembled and in four-legged form when I emerge from the cave as my wolf.

True to Levi's instruction, we hunt first, and then, when our bellies are full of rabbit, we make our way to the meeting point where everyone else will be waiting.

The checkpoint Jadick mentioned turns out to be a campground in Virginia that feels dangerously close to Blackstone's town limits.

Jadick and the rest of the convoy are already there when we arrive. Through a break in the trees at the top of a ridge, I spot tents and canvas rooftops already erected. A cooking fire makes my stomach rumble in response to the aromas. The only other scents on the air are those of the Jades. And my mother. Even so, Levi makes us do three loops around the perimeter, checking for some sign of a trap before he's satisfied it's safe.

When we descend, Jadick is sitting near the fire, surrounded by women. I have to remind myself it's because most of the men are with us, but still—it paints a picture that has me rolling my eyes.

On the fringes, I spot Frankie, and when our eyes lock, I get the impression she agrees with me about Jadick's...methods.

"You made it," Jadick says as Levi and I walk through the camp to where he sits. He doesn't look worried, but that's Jadick. Confident. Too sure of himself to worry.

I tell myself that's the mark of a winner.

But I can still remember my mother telling me during training sessions, "Cocky equals dead."

I don't even realize Levi's shifted back to his human form until he speaks. "Run into any trouble?" he asks.

"None." Jadick's gaze lands on me. "You?"

"A few scouts in the canyon. Nothing we couldn't handle."

"Sounds like a fun story." Jadick snaps his fingers at one of the Jades sitting nearby. Some girl who watches Jadick like he's some sort of god. "Felicia, be a sweetheart and get them something to wear, darling."

"Sure."

She jumps up and hurries to hand over a couple of plastic grocery bags. Levi takes them, and it's all I can do not to bare my teeth at the way her skin brushes his.

Mine.

My wolf is about three seconds from either peeing on him or clawing her tits off. Anything to stake her claim.

Levi turns away from her and gives me a knowing look.

"Come on," he says.

Feeling stiff after our fight last night, I follow him back to the thicker trees and take what clothing he dumps at my feet. He leaves me alone to change, and I listen as he divvies out the remaining clothing with the others who arrived with us.

I listen as he asks about the rest of our men and the answering reports that they've all arrived ahead of us. Everyone who survived is here.

My relief is mixed with sorrow for the lives we lost.

Wind tugs at the ends of my tangled hair as I hurry to

pull on the secondhand jeans and t-shirt. The jeans are tight as hell, and the shirt is stained, but I'm not complaining. I'm grateful for anything that lets me eat food that's been cooked over a flame instead of hunting another rabbit.

When I'm finished, I step out from my little changing area to find my mother waiting. She wears the same thing she always does—fitted cargo pants and a long-sleeve Henley. There's a small cut across her cheek that's nearly healed.

"Tripp called me. I came as soon as I heard." She gives me a quick once-over. "You're okay?"

It's more of a statement. We both know "okay" equals alive to her. Anything else can be healed but not if you're dead.

"I'm fine. You?"

I expect her to brush off my concern, but she doesn't. Instead, she hesitates, and in that brief pause, I see it—something has happened. Something besides the Jades compound being compromised and destroyed. Something besides the lives lost before they could escape with us.

"What is it?" I ask, adrenaline pumping.

As usual, my training kicks in, and my heart rate remains steadily calm in the face of danger.

"It's Kari," she says.

"What about her? Is she—"

She puts up a hand to stop me. "Come. See for yourself."

I follow her back to the fire where Jadick still waits. His entourage has left, and now it's Levi and Tripp sitting with him.

"Did you tell her?" Tripp asks, glancing from me to my mom.

"Only that it's about Kari," my mom says as she takes a seat across the fire from Jadick.

"What happened to Kari?" I demand, refusing to sit.

Jadick doesn't meet my eyes. Levi looks just as confused as I am, which means they haven't told him either.

Tripp sighs. "Here."

He holds out his phone, and I take it, noting he's queued up a video. Levi comes to stand beside me and leans over my shoulder to watch. I press play.

Kari's face fills the screen.

She's gagged, and her cheeks are flushed red and tear-stained.

I draw a shuddering breath then hold it as the camera zooms out to reveal the rest of her. She's tied to a chair. Her hair and clothes are dirty. But there's no blood that I can see.

Not yet.

A sign rests in her lap.

On it, someone has scrawled words in black marker: *Dear Mac, Will trade for Jadick Clemons. 24 hours or this deal dies.*

After a beat, the camera pans around to reveal Thiago. He offers a sadistic sort of wave that's friendly if you're into serial killers and narcissistic assholes. The camera focuses on him until the picture goes black and the video ends.

"Fuck," Levi says and moves away to pace.

"When was this sent?" I demand.

"About three hours ago," Tripp says.

Forcing myself to breathe, I look at Jadick. "Dirk gave you up."

"It seems that way."

"He put my name on it," I say, "which means he knows I'm with you."

"It also means you have a target on your back as big as his," Levi practically snarls.

"Relax, man," Tripp tells him. "It just means he's using her friendship with Kari against her."

Levi rounds on him, but my mother interrupts.

"Tripp is right. Thiago knows using Kari as bait only works on the people who care about her most. And that's Mac."

I want to be mad, but my mother's right, and all that matters now is Kari.

"What are we going to do?" I ask, desperation leaking into my voice.

"We're going to give him what he wants," Jadick says.

I watch him, skeptical and wary about what he actually means.

"And what's that?" I ask.

He shrugs like it's nothing and says, "Me."

"So, you're going to challenge him?" I say.

"Don't be naïve, Mac. It's a trap."

"So, then what—?"

"Relax. He's showing his hand like I said he would."

"And what hand is that?" I ask.

"He's obviously decided I'm more valuable to him

than Kari. Now we know he's willing to do anything to get to me. We can use this."

Jadick sounds so confident, so smooth. I'm not sure whether to find comfort in that or be even more worried about how this will end.

Levi is tensely silent and hasn't taken his eyes off the fire for long enough that I wonder if he's hypnotized by it—or maybe he's that determined to tune us out.

"So, you challenge him then," Tripp is saying when I force myself to tune back into the conversation, "winner becomes alpha."

"If it were that simple, I would have challenged him the moment our father died," Jadick says.

"Jadick's right," Levi says, finally joining in the conversation though he doesn't look at me. "Thiago has no honor. He won't fight fair."

"Then neither do we," I say.

My mom nods because, in this, we agree.

Jadick merely grins.

"You have an idea," I say.

"Of course." He glances between us all, and I can see that he enjoys keeping us on the hook like this.

"Well?" my mother demands. "Spit it out."

"Thiago will be expecting a direct assault because he knows we *do* have honor," Jadick says. "Instead, we use the Jades to infiltrate the city. I have a small contingent of men still loyal to me there. Informants, soldiers—they'll help. We'll neutralize the men we already know my brother will have positioned out of sight, ready to shoot us in the back."

Levi doesn't answer. Something's wrong. I can see it every time he looks at Jadick. I just don't know what.

"We don't have the numbers," Tripp says, shaking his head to dismiss the idea. "We were already outnumbered before, but we lost too many in the attack. Not to mention morale... We lost women and children, man."

His quiet outrage speaks volumes. I can feel the heat of my own fury coursing through my veins. I remember the faces of those I watched fall as the hangar caved in around us.

"Then we'll get the numbers," Jadick says.

He's still so calm, and my rage points at him now.

"From where? And when?" I demand.

"Vicki has mafia contacts," Jadick says, "And I have some friends in Hawley pack who might—"

"Hawley pack doesn't even exist anymore," I say. "They're all Lone Wolf pack now. And their alphas are a day's drive from here."

"We'll send teams," he says. "One to the Lone Wolf alphas. Another to the Mafia pack."

"We don't have that kind of time," I say, frustration mounting. "Kari needs us now. Thiago won't wait around. We have to respond before the deadline, or he'll only up the stakes, which means hurting Kari or worse. You have to let me bring you in."

"I'm not going to just walk into a trap," Jadick says, condescension dripping from his words. "That might be how you do things, but it's not smart enough to win this war."

My hands ball into fists.

Before I can use them on his privileged little face, Levi stands. "I'll go."

I stare up at him, confused. "What?"

He looks at me. "Thiago sent you to hunt down who killed his father. He said he'll let Kari go if you give him that person. Take me in. Trade me for Kari."

"Levi..."

It's what I wanted. Or what I set out to do, anyway. But now, after everything that's happened, I can't imagine turning Levi over to Thiago. Or to anyone.

"I can't let you do that," I say, pain twisting my words.

"We can't ignore his message," he says. I'm too torn to appreciate that he actually agrees with my plan—for the first time maybe ever.

"You're not *letting* me do anything," he says, his words an exact reminder of the ones I'd tossed at him that first night I tried to take him down.

But I can't find humor in it.

"You'd be walking directly into his trap," my mother says. "He'll have snipers ready."

"Vicki's right," Tripp says. "That's the stupidest move we could make. We need to be smart about this."

"We need to stop sitting on our asses," Levi snaps, except that he's glaring at Jadick as he says it.

Jadick gets to his feet, his air of nonchalance gone. Now, his jaw is hardened, and his eyes are obsidian stones. "I'm the alpha heir, and I'll say when we go."

"You're not an alpha yet," Levi says.

There's a tension between them that feels bigger than this conversation. Tripp catches my eye and gives a small shake of his head, basically telling me to stay out of it.

"Are you really going to cut me out of this, brother? After the partnership we've had? After everything I've done for you." His gaze flicks to me. "She's alive because of me."

"What?" I ask.

Even my mother looks confused now.

"Mac's not your concern any longer," Levi says in a hard voice.

"She's clouding your judgment," Jadick says. "Distracting you from our real goals."

"Our goal has always been about saving innocent lives," Levi says. His voice is rising now. His temper leaking out through cracked edges. "Your own sister is that innocent life in this scenario, and yet you continue to sit around pretending you've got everything under control."

"Watch it, Levi. I'm not one of your Jades you can just order around."

"That's right," Levi snaps. "*My* Jades. *I* am their alpha."

"You serve at my leisure," Jadick says.

I can't help wondering what the hell that means, but Levi's eyes flash, and he leans closer, getting in Jadick's face.

"Leisure is the perfect word, isn't it? All you do is sit on your ass while everyone else does the dirty work."

"You are an alpha for the sole reason that I never challenged you," Jadick says coldly. "Remember that, and remember what you're fighting for. Or who."

This time, it's Levi who glances at me.

"Believe me," Levi says, "I haven't forgotten."

Then he walks away, disappearing into the darkness that's fallen around camp.

Jadick lets him go without a word.

Finally, he takes his seat again, clapping Tripp on the back and sliding right back into his cheery persona. "Who wants a beer?" Jadick asks.

Tripp doesn't answer.

"I'm going to bed," my mother says and abruptly stands and walks off.

She doesn't go after Levi. I wonder if I should follow her.

"Mac?"

I look up to find Jadick holding a can out toward me. Tripp eyes me across the fire. I can't read his expression—or more specifically, I can't figure out who he's frustrated at most right now. But I don't wait around to find out.

"See you tomorrow," I say and leave Jadick and Tripp to strategize a plan I never plan to follow.

CHAPTER
TWENTY

Levi's long gone by the time I try to catch his scent. The tracker in me could still hunt him down, but after what just happened back there, I need time alone to think. Especially now. Turning away from Levi's trail, I head into the woods, crashing through brush, uncaring where the path leads. The sliver of moon overhead provides a dim light, though my wolf can see the way easily enough without it.

I walk until I come to a wide creek. The rushing of the water echoes around me, and in the chaos of that noise, I search for clarity.

Adrenaline pumps, my thoughts consumed by the video. Thiago's demand replays over and over in my mind. If I don't deliver Jadick, he'll hurt Kari. I know it. Just as I know I'll never convince Jadick to come back with me.

There has to be another way.

But the only other option is Levi, and I can't bring myself to ask him to sacrifice himself. Not even for Kari.

Maybe a few days ago, I could have done it. But too much has happened since I left the pack. Too many crimes have been forgiven between us. I can't lose him again, not this way.

A branch cracks, and I whirl to see Tripp coming toward me in the darkness.

He holds up his hands in mock surrender.

"Just me," he says. "Don't shoot."

I turn back to the creek, staring at where the water breaks over a rock. "I figured you'd still be at camp, plotting war games with Jadick."

"Your mother agreed to go to Franco in the morning. To ask for backup." He sighs. "Jadick's gone back to drinking with his fan club. He considers it settled for now."

"I bet he does."

"It's not going to work."

I frown. "What are you talking about?"

"You have that look in your eye. The one you get when you think you can just talk someone into something. I'm telling you, Mac. It won't work. He won't do this—not for you and not for Kari."

I turn to look at him. "She's his sister."

"He's out here trying to strategize how to kill his own brother. Do you think family ties matter to any of them?"

"They're not all like that."

He doesn't answer.

"I know you don't like her," I begin.

"I don't trust her," he corrects. "There's a difference."

"Is there?"

"It's not personal. I don't know her well enough to not like her."

"Exactly."

He sighs. "If an entire batch of something is exposed to poison but only two of the three become contaminated, which results do you suspect—the majority or the minority?"

I shove him playfully. "She's not a science experiment, you nerd."

But he doesn't let up with the somber expression. "Exactly. These are people's lives we're talking about. And I don't fuck around with the lives of my friends."

"Kari's different," I say stubbornly. "You don't know her like I do."

He doesn't answer, and I know we're just going to agree to disagree—again. I might have argued if I didn't want to be past all this once and for all. To have my friend back.

"Anyway, Jadick's a dick, but he's not out here trying to kill us like Thiago is."

Tripp looks entirely unconvinced as he says, "He's a Clemons, Mac. They all are."

CHAPTER
TWENTY-ONE

Tripp walks me back to camp in silence. Deep down, I know he's only making sure I don't do something crazy like run off to save Kari alone. But he doesn't say as much, and I'm grateful. It lets me pretend he's just here to be my friend instead of a babysitter.

He stops in front of a large tent. "Your mom made up a sleeping bag for you," he says.

I nod. "Thanks for walking with me."

"Sure." He hesitates. "See you tomorrow."

"See you."

He doesn't leave until I climb into the tent and zip it closed.

My mother's already asleep. She stirs as I climb into the extra sleeping bag.

"You okay?" she mumbles sleepily.

"Fine, Mom."

She mumbles, "The enemy of my enemy is my friend, Mac. Remember that."

I hold back a sigh. Even in her sleep, she's quoting cliches at me like some kind of wise woman.

"Good night, Mom."

"G'night."

I listen to the symphony of night insects and do my best to count time as it passes. The longer I lie here, the more resolved I become to my crazy-ass plan. Offering myself in exchange for Kari is possibly the dumbest move I can make. It's also futile.

Thiago will never go for it.

He doesn't want me.

The only person he'll let Kari go for is Jadick.

And maybe Levi since he knows Levi will lead him to Jadick. That's why he let me go after Levi in the first place. Torturing Dirk was only the prelude—a show of what will happen if I dare bring him my mate.

But... if I can make the exchange public—offer myself in front of the pack—I might have a shot at making it work. It'll mean confessing to Crigger's murder, which carries a death sentence. But I can't think of another way. I meant what I said to Levi last night. He took my choices away. At least now, as bleak as the options are, I can choose my fate. Even if it means dying for that choice.

I spend what feels like hours lying here trying to think of something else.

In the end, there is only me.

My death for Kari's life.

It's horrific but it beats carrying the weight of her

death on my shoulders for the rest of my life. I can't bear it, and I know that because the deaths of the Jades we left behind already threaten to consume me.

I can't take one more.

My mother's snores offer more than enough noise to cover the shuffling sounds my clothes make as I dress and slip outside. She doesn't stir as I move past her and into the night air. How that woman can sleep so heavily in her line of work is beyond me. But tonight, I'm glad for it.

I pause long enough to press a feather-light kiss to my mother's cheek.

I love you.

I don't dare speak the words aloud. It'll have to be enough that I kept her safely out of the conflict. Even as I think it, though, I know the opposite will be true. She'll be angrier that I did this without her than the fact that I did it at all.

Guards are stationed around the camp. I can't see them, but I can sense them.

My wolf catches their scents easily enough on the wind, and I pick my way slowly through the camp to avoid their detection.

After what feels like forever, I leave the last of the Jades behind me.

Ahead, a narrow trail snakes its way through thick forest. The road would be faster. But it's too risky.

I can take this until dawn.

By then, I'll have enough of a head start to—

A figure looms before me.

"Going somewhere?"

I swallow a scream and lock eyes with Levi.

"Dammit," I hiss. "You almost gave me a heart attack."

"You're the one sneaking around camp in the middle of the night. Shouldn't I be the one scared?"

Tears burn my eyes at the sight of him. I had hoped to spare myself this particular goodbye. In fact, looking at him, I know I can't bring myself to say it.

"I'm not stopping you," I tell him. "Scream if you have to."

Doing my best to seem unaffected, I start for the trail, but he falls into step beside me.

"I think I'll just walk it off."

"What are you doing?" I ask sharply.

"Coming with you. What the hell do you think?"

I stop and turn to face him. "Levi, you can't." My voice nearly breaks on the words.

"Why? Because Jadick said so?"

He's angry, but I know it's meant for Jadick and not me.

"I don't know everything that's happened between you two," I start.

"And you don't need to. All you need to know is that I agree with you about answering Thiago's demand."

"Jadick wants to wait," I remind him.

"Jadick is a coward," he snarls. I blink at the vehemence in his words. He straightens and calms. "But we don't need him."

"What are you going to do?" I ask, finally realizing what he means by joining me.

"I'm not doing anything," he says. "*You* are going to

hand me over to Thiago, get Kari back, and then tell the others what I've done so they can come and get me out of there, hopefully before Thiago cuts me into tiny pieces."

"You're counting on Jadick to rescue you? I don't know if that's such a safe bet."

"No, Mac." He takes my hand, squeezing it and sending a zing of pleasure through me at the simple touch. "I'm counting on you."

I shake my head, ready to refuse his insane plan. "It's impossible," I say. "We haven't had time to plan it or think through all the ways it could go wrong—"

"Oh? And what was your plan?" he asks.

I don't answer.

"Run back there alone? Beg him to let Kari go out of the kindness of his heart? You have no leverage without me, Mac."

"I have myself," I say quietly.

He looks stricken, and I know he's realized what I meant to do.

"You were going to die," he says, his voice hoarse.

"I was going to save Kari," I say. "And end the standoff. Buy you all more time to do ... whatever it is you're going to do."

He stares at me like I've just slapped him. Finally, he shakes his head, snapping out of it. "Thiago would never go for it. He'll throw you out on your ass. Or maybe kill you for fun, but it wouldn't help Kari."

"It would if I made it public," I say. "Confess," I shove the word out, and he goes pale. "Tell everyone I killed Crigger."

"Make it impossible for him to do anything but execute you," he says, his voice rough with anger. "You really are insane, you know that?"

"If it were you in that cell, I would do the same," I say quietly.

"If it were me in that cell, you would leave me and never look back," he says. "Because that's what I would want for you. To be safe. Happy."

"That's the problem, Levi." I stop walking and face him, "Don't you see? I could never be happy without you."

His gaze softens.

He steps closer, pressing his warm palm to my flushed cheek. I lean into his touch, closing my eyes and trying to block out the horror of what has brought us together again. For just a moment, I want to pretend it's just us, finding our way back.

When I open my eyes again, the reality of what lies ahead is too harsh to pretend away. A single tear slips down my cheek, and he brushes it away with his thumb.

"I'm going to make this right," he says. "You have to let me do this. For you. For what I did—before."

"You were protecting me," I mumble.

"Let me protect you now," he says.

And I can only nod and give in. I've never been any good at telling Levi no.

WE SHIFT and walk until dawn as wolves. Mostly to access our senses more fully, avoiding patrols and getting through the boundary line undetected, but it also keeps me from saying or doing something drastic. My wolf whines at being told to keep her paws to herself, but giving myself over to Levi now will only make everything harder. I can't afford to give in to my emotions, no matter how badly I want to. Once we have Kari back, maybe then I can figure out where I really stand with the man beside me.

The journey to Blackstone isn't far, but it's painfully slow. We stick to the high ground and the thickets, using all our senses to be sure we aren't tracked or spotted by scouts. I have no doubt Thiago's got all of the pack lands on high alert after that video he sent us.

The closer we get, the more I start to wonder if the others were right; this plan is insane. We're so far past outnumbered, it's pathetic.

But it's not about numbers, I remind myself. Not when it comes to Thiago.

Levi sticks close, his fur brushing mine often as we make our way. I can feel his worry, but more than that, I feel his resolve. He's all in. With this plan. With me.

I think of what Jadick said to him last night. About me clouding his judgment. And I cross my fingers I'm not leading him to his doom.

The outskirts of town come into view just as the sun clears the treetops. We crest the final hill overlooking the valley of Blackstone, and Levi stops. He nods at a stand of trees, and we shift back to our human forms and put on the clothes we've carried in our mouths.

"Here." Levi holds out a length of rope.

"What's this?"

"I'm your prisoner," he says. "We have to make it believable."

"Levi..."

"Don't overthink it, Mac." He comes to stand in front of me, his hands squeezing my upper arms. "This will work. Kari will be safe."

"What about you?"

"We talked about this." His voice is gentle, reassuring. And I hate it. "Wait until you and Kari are safely away, and then we'll figure something out."

"I can't do this," I say, my voice breaking. "I already got enough people killed—"

"No," he says. "Those deaths are not your fault, Mac. Thiago did that."

"I was the one who hunted you—"

"And he used that to hurt the people around us. Thiago's fucked up choices are his, not yours."

I sigh.

He cups my cheeks, wiping at the place where tears would have fallen if I'd only let them. "Stop blaming yourself," he whispers. "Besides, I was a dick for rejecting you. Being tortured by Thiago is the least of what I deserve, right?"

His lips curve at his own horrible joke, and I feel a smile tugging at my mouth in spite of it all.

"Actually, in my revenge plot, I'm the one torturing you."

"Oh, that sounds way more sexy," he says, leaning in to trail kisses along my throat.

"Exactly." I close my eyes at the intensity of pleasure but force my voice to remain light. "Torture's only sexy if you let your prisoner go to the bathroom before things get messy."

"Noted. I will try my best to remember that for next time," he says, breath tickling my neck as he continues to kiss his way closer to my mouth.

"And maybe consider a menu other than drugged lasagna," I tell him.

He pulls back to frown at me. "What are you talking about?"

I roll my eyes. "Okay, we're still pretending."

"Mac," he says, very carefully. "None of the food was drugged. Or at least, not by me."

I stare at him, trying to decide whether I believe him. I kind of hate that we've come far enough to make out but not far enough for me to know if he'd lie about something like that. "Well, someone did," I say.

He lets out a growl and then steps back and punches the tree beside him. His knuckles crack against the bark, but the only one who comes out injured is him. Blood coats his knuckles, and he paces away, shaking his head against the pain.

The outburst is out of place, which only makes me worry.

"Whoa, chill. It made sense. The Jades don't trust me," I start to say, but he cuts me off.

"I questioned Grey extensively before we left the compound. None of the Jades were ever alone with your food. The only two people who were are sitting around that campfire trying to talk you out of doing exactly what we're about to do."

My blood ices over, and my heart threatens to crack at the possibility of what he's implying. Jadick, I can accept. He's a cocky douche who's only looking out for himself. And I'm sure, if I think hard enough, I can come up with a hundred reasons why he'd think killing me would help serve his cause.

But Tripp?

I can't even fathom the idea of that kind of betrayal.

"Tripp would never," I whisper.

Levi groans and runs a hand through his hair. "We don't have time for this kind of suspicion." He closes the distance, his energy chaotic now. "Mac, listen, we need to keep moving. We're too exposed out here. Let's just get Kari, and then we'll figure this all out, okay?"

"I can't rescue you without help, Levi. And if I can't trust Tripp—"

"Go to your mother. She has contacts you can use. People outside our group."

"She has business associates. My mother doesn't have friends, Levi. Why do you think she allied with you guys, knowing Jadick Clemons is running the show? She hates him. But she doesn't have anyone better to support."

He squeezes his eyes shut, and when he opens them again, I find a desperation I've never seen in them before. "We'll figure it out. We just have to keep moving. If we're spotted here—"

A shot rings out, and sharp pain lances through my shoulder. I gasp, and Levi roars, shoving me down. I hit the ground with a thud that I feel all the way down my spine, but even before I can open my mouth to cry out, the heaviness descends. My limbs weaken, and my tongue becomes a lead weight in my mouth. I can't even summon up the energy to be afraid as I watch Levi jerk in sudden pain and fall beside me.

He lands on his side, a dart protruding from his neck, and our eyes meet as scouts rush in to surround us.

"Targets down," someone says. A male voice I don't recognize.

A scream echoes inside the confines of my own mind. I am paralyzed against everything except my own emotions.

Fear.

Frustration.

Defeat.

Exhaustion presses heavily against my eyelids. Levi tries to speak but only grunts. I look back at him, unable to form the words to tell him how much I love him before the pull of darkness sucks me under and sweeps me away.

CHAPTER
TWENTY-TWO

I wake chilled to the bone and very aware that, underneath the thin sheet someone has draped over me, I'm naked. Inhaling sharply, I open my eyes and sit up, scanning the room where I've woken. It's bland and sparsely furnished. Not a bedroom, despite the narrow bed I'm lying in. Stainless steel shelving and a bedside tray to match are the only furniture beyond the thin mattress. Across the small room, a closed door leads... I don't know where.

Through a hazy mind, I try to think. To get my bearings.

The last memory I can summon involves being shot with a dart laced with a drug strong enough to drop me where I stood. Not an easy feat when your target is a werewolf whose metabolism runs three to four times faster than a normal human. And then, men crowding around us, shouting at one another to take us into custody.

I don't know who they are, but my bet is on a certain

douchebag alpha with a soft spot for sibling torture.

What I do know is I'm alone.

Levi isn't here.

That realization leaves a hollow fear coating my insides.

I scramble up, tossing the cover aside. Nudity isn't a new concept. And I have far worse problems than lack of clothing right now.

The door's locked, but I'm not deterred.

Stepping back, I call on my wolf.

She stirs slowly. I breathe a sigh of relief that they haven't bothered to mute her like Thiago did to me the last time he had me drugged. But before I can call my beast to the surface and shift, the lock clicks, and the door swings open.

I back away as Thiago walks in.

He looks me over, his gaze lingering on my breasts until I'm more uncomfortable than I am angry. He plants himself between me and the door. Behind him, a trio of guards waits just outside.

"Move," I say, my voice hard.

"Sure," he says breezily. "But first, maybe you'd like to explain to me where my brother is hiding. My men have searched high and low on those slopes and turned up nothing besides you and your lovesick little runaway."

"What have you done with Levi?"

Just the mere mention of him has me twisting in knots. My wolf surges, ready to show herself and rip Thiago to shreds if he's done something to harm our mate.

But just like I am singly focused on Levi, Thiago's

clearly not ready to let the subject of Jadick go.

"You tell me where Jadick's hiding, and I'll take you to Levi," he says. When I don't answer, his grin broadens as if he's telling some sort of inside joke as he adds, "I'll show you mine if you show me yours."

"If you've hurt Levi at all—"

"I haven't yet," he snaps, smile vanishing. His expression strains as he snarls, "But refuse to answer me and that can change. Now, where is Jadick hiding, and what is his plan of attack?"

I stare back at him.

"He's not here," I say, and Thiago laughs harshly.

"Stop lying," he hisses.

"I'm not."

"We can do this the easy way or the hard way."

"Jadick isn't here," I repeat, louder this time.

Frustration heats my skin until the chilled room doesn't even register anymore. Thiago looks just as angry, if not more. He isn't convinced.

"He didn't come with us," I say. "We did this on our own."

It's a hard truth to admit, mostly because it means we're idiots. A failed plan with no backup and no rescue in sight. Thiago has us now, and he can do what he wants.

Except he never wanted Levi. Or me.

That much is clear from the disappointment clinging to him now.

"All right," he says, straightening and squaring his shoulders as if accepting something unsavory. "The hard way it is."

He turns to the guards. "Bring her in."

I back away, returning to the bed and grabbing the sheet. Wolves are used to nudity, but only when it means we're shifting. I don't exactly want to negotiate for my life—or Kari's—with every bargaining chip I own on full display.

Better to leave some of the mystery alive.

Wrapping the sheet like a makeshift dress, I tuck the ends together and then stand ready for whoever Thiago has summoned.

Kari steps into the open doorway, and I forget all about the sheet or trying to hide my vulnerability.

She's here. Alive.

That's all that matters.

"Kari," I breathe, relief threatening to buckle my limbs. I rush forward and wrap her in a tight hug. "I was so worried. Are you okay?" I pull back to study her. The dark circles underneath her eyes. A scratch along her left cheek that's just beginning to scab over. And a bruise along her jaw that's faded to a dark purple. All of these are recent. They have to be, considering how fast wolves heal.

"Did he—"

I can't even finish my sentence. My rage for Thiago is so completely beyond the ability to form words.

"I'm okay," Kari says.

Behind her, Thiago closes the door, offering us a moment of privacy. I'm surprised by the generosity, but then my worry for Kari takes over, and I drink in the moment, knowing it might be my last. Or hers.

"Come here." I pull her back to the bed, and we sit.

"Tell me everything. I saw the video he made. He tied you up. I just... I'm sorry I took so long getting back here. But I found him."

It makes me sick to say the words—like they're the solution instead of an entirely new horrific problem.

"Who?" she asks, eyes lighting with hope.

"Levi," I say, cringing at what I'm offering here.

But seeing Kari battered and bruised at the mercy of a monster like Thiago leaves me no choice. I can't just leave her here. She doesn't deserve this. No one does.

"Levi?" she repeats, frowning.

"Yes, Thiago said I had to find your father's killer. He's the one I saw in that warehouse."

"Levi didn't kill my dad."

Her words startle me. How would she know? "That doesn't matter. Thiago has to honor our arrangement," I say. "He'll let you go."

"And what about you?"

"What about me?"

Her hands grip mine tightly. She leans in, eyes beseeching me. "Thiago wants Jadick," she says. "If you just give up where in the city he's hidden himself, when he plans to strike, I know Thiago will let you go."

"He doesn't plan to strike," I say.

"Mac," she says, her chin wobbling with the threat of tears. "I don't know what he'll do if you keep lying to him."

I shudder, my gaze flicking to the bruise along her jaw.

He'll do that and worse, I have no doubt.

"But I'm not lying. Jadick wouldn't come. He said it was too risky. That we needed more time, more men—"

"Dammit, Mac." The hardness in her voice stops me more than the words. "Don't you want to save me?"

I stare at her, shocked. "Of course I do. That's why I brought Levi—"

"Oh, screw Levi. He's as hell-bent on protecting you as you are of him."

I stare at her.

The flicker of darkness that flashes in her eyes isn't something I recognize at all.

"How do you know what Levi is hell-bent on doing?"

She scowls.

"Kari."

My heart pounds.

A slow dread crawls over my skin. It creeps beneath the sheet I've wrapped so tightly around me, hooking its claws into my flesh. I know its name even before I find the courage to voice it: suspicion.

Kari doesn't waver.

Her spine is straight, her gaze sharpened to a razor point.

It's that directness stabbing straight into my heart that makes me want to weep.

"How do you know what Levi is doing?" I repeat, my voice cracking as my heart begins to break. "And where did you get that bruise, really?"

She starts to answer, another lie clear on the tip of her tongue.

"I gave up my freedom for you," I whisper, and she finally drops the mask.

Her expression twists.

Gone is the terrified desperation. In its place is cold cruelty far beyond anything I've witnessed from Thiago. She stands and, eyes still locked on me, calls over her shoulder, "She's not going to give him up. I'm done here."

The door opens.

Thiago reappears, flanked by guards.

I stare, wide-eyed and disbelieving of the realizations threatening to drown me.

Thiago smirks. "I'm nothing compared to him, you know," he says.

I blink, confused. "You mean Jadick."

Kari backs toward Thiago, a clear alliance. Even so, I can hardly believe what I'm seeing.

"He's a monster," Thiago says. "Why else would we be going to such lengths to stop him. You could help us."

"No, I think you're much, much worse," I say, my voice hoarse.

This can't be happening.

Levi.

I have to get to Levi.

"You must not have spent much time with him, then," Thiago says.

It's a taunt.

He wants me to protest, to argue that I have spent plenty of time with him and know exactly where Jadick is now. I almost give in to it. There's no reason not to. I owe the man nothing. Less than nothing, in fact, for his abandonment of us. Of his own sister. Though, I wonder if he knew what I didn't all along.

Still.

He's sitting in a camp with my mother and Tripp and the rest of the Jades who trusted him enough to follow him here.

And I won't sacrifice them.

Not even for Levi.

Not even for myself.

"You're all monsters," I say, glancing at Kari.

The Kari I knew would wince. She'd be hurt at the accusation. But this one merely rolls her eyes and turns to Thiago. "If she isn't going to give us Jadick's location, we're done here." She turns to the security team waiting in the hall. "Dispatch more teams. Keep scouring the woods. Widen the perimeter. He's out there, and I want him found. Today."

Her voice is cold and demanding.

"All this time, you were helping him," I say. "Not a prisoner. A willing participant."

Kari turns to me, impatience dripping from a sour expression I barely recognize on her face. "I'm my father's daughter, Mac. What did you expect?"

"You were my best friend."

Something passes over her face. Regret? Sorrow? I try to identify it before the darkness creeps in again, but I can't read her like I used to.

Actually, I never could, I realize now.

"That's the thing, Mac. I was never the girl you thought you knew."

The truth of this moment—of Kari's deception—is a knife in my back. It hurts so much worse than anything I've been through up to this moment.

"I won't help you," I say, my chin lifting in a resolve that's unnecessary. They've already realized they'll get nothing from me. Not willingly, anyway. But I have to take a stand against the pain of Kari's betrayal.

"You don't have to be willing in order to help," Thiago says. "Remember the warehouse?"

My eyes snap to his. "What about the warehouse?" I demand.

Kari sighs.

"She can still offer information," Thiago tells Kari, ignoring me. "There are other ways of taking what she doesn't want to give."

Torture.

Kari pauses, and my throat constricts as I realize how quickly the tables have turned. Now, she holds my life in her hands. And I wait while she decides whether I'm worth saving.

Finally, she shakes her head, flicking a dismissive hand in my direction. "Turn her loose. Maybe she'll lead us to Jadick, though I doubt she's stupid enough to fall for it."

"And the mate?" Thiago asks.

Levi.

Kari looks me over, still considering. "Hang on to him. He is the leader of a rebellion, after all." She looks at me. "You're going to leave and never come back, do you understand me? Because if you do, you'll collect your mate in pieces, limb by severed fucking limb."

CHAPTER
TWENTY-THREE

My gut feels as if someone's punched a gaping hole through it. I can't wrap my head around what's happening. Kari has betrayed me—betrayed us all. Everything I thought I knew about her—about all of this—is a lie. She isn't in need of saving. Hell, she isn't worth saving. She's the villain in this story. I can see that now as I stare between her and Thiago. He's a monster; there's no question about that. But he's following her lead. That means she's in charge here. A Clemons, through and through, considering the lengths she's gone to try and lure Jadick out. To manipulate me into bringing him to her.

Out of all the siblings, Kari's the one I should worry about.

And I've just delivered Levi right into her hands.

The one person she knows she can use to control me.

Otherwise, I'd wrap my hands around her throat and

squeeze until her eyes popped out of her skull. If only to end this.

Now, all that matters is saving Levi.

Regardless of what's happened in our past, I refuse to leave him here, in the hands of these monsters.

My wolf rises swiftly to the surface, tearing my skin apart in her haste to get free. My bones pop and lengthen, and I drop to all fours, baring my teeth at both of my captors.

If Kari thinks I'm going to just walk out of here without a fight, she never really knew me at all either.

Thiago grins—he, at least, saw this coming.

His shift is nearly as fast as mine.

I snarl and lunge for Kari, but Thiago is quick. The moment his paws settle on the cold floor, he shoves me back. My claws rake over his fur, opening shallow gashes along his right side.

He doesn't even flinch as he counters my movements and goes on the offensive. He's trained well—but I'm better.

Unfortunately, he has an entire team of soldiers on his side.

Our fight spills into the hall, and I do my best to keep from becoming surrounded. Unfortunately, that's a losing battle with so many opponents.

Thiago's the only one of them who fights me as a wolf. The rest of them use guns, and I can only hope they're still armed with sleeping darts rather than actual bullets.

One of the men fires.

I turn to look at where the shot went, and Thiago rams

into me, sending me careening. I crash through a wall and shake myself against the dazed feeling it leaves behind. Aches and pains scream for attention, but I force myself up again.

I cannot let him beat me.

Behind him and his wall of brutes, Kari watches us.

She doesn't look invested in the least. More curious than anything. Maybe even bored. That ignites my fury all over again, and I crouch at Thiago, ready to spring past him toward her.

Before I can move, a roar fills the air. Something moves beside me.

Levi.

He leaps from his bed and shifts. Thiago doesn't even wait for him to complete the change before he strikes. I'm forced to intervene, knocking Thiago away from Levi before any damage is done.

Then, Levi and I are both dodging darts along with Thiago's teeth.

"Don't shoot Thiago, you idiots," Kari snaps at them.

The men stop firing.

We escape into the hall, and Kari backs away, clearly unwilling to join the fight.

Fine.

I'll give her no choice.

With a snap of my teeth, I slip past the closest guard and charge at Kari. My own blood pulses in my ears as I accept what I'm about to do: kill my friend. But Kari slips out of reach, dancing away and then running for a door at the end of the hall.

I chase, listening to the sounds of Thiago and Levi fighting behind me. Thiago snarls, and then their claws click on the hard floor as they follow my lead.

Kari slams through the door, and I tumble out behind her, narrowly missing her calf as we both pass into bright sunlight.

I glance around wildly, trying to get my bearings.

We're on the steps of the alpha house, far left of the main entrance. A side door with more than enough visibility from the street where a crowd has gathered.

At the sight of us, their voices lift in screams and cries for justice.

I falter, confused.

Kari stares at them, just as bewildered, and it takes me a long moment to realize they aren't here at her bidding.

If she didn't do this, who did?

Something slams into me from behind.

Not something, someone.

Thiago's teeth latch onto my hind leg, and I howl in pain as he rips me open. My legs give out, and I tumble hard against the concrete.

Thiago comes in for another bite, and I manage to fight him off. Over his shoulder, I watch as a dart strikes Levi in the hind leg. His eyes widen, blazing with surprise—and pain.

Then he snarls and comes for Thiago, ripping him off me with his claws.

Another shot hits Levi.

His eyelids begin to droop. His movements slow.

The crowd roars, and through the blood pumping in

my ears, I have no idea if they're cheering for us—or for them.

A third dart hits Levi.

He falls, hard, eyes closed before he hits the ground.

I whimper, pulling myself to my feet, wincing at the pain from the wound Thiago gave me.

If I don't do something, they'll put me down next.

The shift hurts this time. When I return to my human form, I'm covered in blood, and not all of it's mine. Healing will be much slower this way, but there are more important things than my torn body.

"You all came for a killer," I scream at the crowd.

They're closer now, pressing in toward us with angry expressions. Some carry signs scrawled with words like "Justice for Crigger" and "Death to Romantics."

At my words, they roar back at me, urging me to give them what they want.

"There," I scream, pointing at Thiago, who's already stalking toward me like a predator ready to finish off its prey.

He halts, mid-attack.

The crowd turns to him, shock muting their cries.

"*He's* responsible for Crigger's death," I yell at them. "And he's not the only one."

My gaze swings to Kari. Our eyes meet.

I can't help the pain in my chest as I summon the words that will condemn her, once and for all, to our entire pack. Words I can never take back.

I look back at the crowd through eyes blurred with tears.

Movement ripples through them. I don't have time to see what's caused the sudden chaos of bodies being abruptly shoved aside. It doesn't matter anyway.

This is all about to end.

Before I can speak, a loud crack splits the air, and I whip my head toward the sound. Thiago falls at my feet, his massive form a mess of blood and flesh and tissue.

Then I look up, past him to where Kari stands with a gun.

No darts. Just bullets.

She meets my eyes.

There's not a shred of remorse in her gaze.

I don't move.

I can't.

Behind me, someone screams my name.

"Mac!"

It breaks the spell, and Kari blinks. She turns to the crowd.

"Mac is right," she tells them in a voice I've never heard her use before. Cold authority rings out in every note. "As you know, she was given the incredible task of hunting down my father's killer. And now, thanks to her, we know the truth. My brother, Thiago, has been working against my family for some time now. He had my father killed and even imprisoned me so that no one could challenge him."

The crowd ripples with unease.

I stare at the gun Kari still holds at her side, heart thudding. On my left, Levi lies still from the darts. Considering how well they worked the first time, I know he won't be getting up anytime soon. But if Kari so much as raises that gun in his direction, I won't hesitate to put myself between them.

"Mac is a hero," Kari declares.

The crowd cheers, pulling my attention back to them. To her.

What is she doing?

She meets my eyes with a sly smile that is more foreign than frightening. Who is this girl? Where is my friend?

Gone, her eyes seem to say.

"Mac deserves a hero's reception," she adds.

The crowd responds in kind, clapping and reaching for me now.

I back away from them, toward Kari.

She says something to her guards. I can't hear the words over the crowd, but they move toward Levi, and my heart leaps.

"Get away from him," I scream at them.

They ignore me, and I take a step forward, ready to fight them off.

The crowd has pressed in close now. Hands grab at me, and I shake them off. A strong grip closes over my wrist. I yank, but the voice in my ear stills me.

"Mac, it's me."

Tripp

I twist to look at him. "What are you doing here?"

My breath catches, and I start to glance around for the others. For Jadick.

"Getting you out of here," he says in a low voice.

"We have to get Levi," I insist.

"Get him inside," Kari yells, and I look up to see the security team hauling Levi's unconscious wolf back toward the door.

I struggle to free myself from Tripp's grasp, but Kari turns and pins me with a look that stops me cold.

"Remember what I said, Mac. Don't come back here. Not unless you want your mate returned in pieces."

The crowd doesn't hear her, they're too busy yelling about Thiago and Crigger and whatever lies Kari has made them believe about all of this. Tripp pulls me away. I stumble, my eyes flinging from Kari to Levi and back again.

A cry lodges in my throat.

I can't leave, not like this. Not without him.

"Mac," Tripp warns, his voice sharp.

Kari glances upward at something behind her and nods.

Still struggling against his attempt to move me, I shriek as the concrete beside me suddenly cracks open with the force of a bullet.

"Mac!" Tripp's grip on me tightens as a second shot whizzes past my ear.

Someone in the crowd screams.

Tripp doesn't ask again. Instead, he grabs me and lifts me off my feet, carrying me off into the throng of people. They part for us, letting us pass, but not before a third bullet finally finds its mark.

Pain explodes in my shoulder.

I jerk violently, and Tripp nearly drops me.

He curses, but I barely hear it over the roar of voices—

and my own blood pounding in my ears.

Pain spreads, paralyzing me, until I hang like a sack of potatoes over Tripp's shoulder. He hisses out a strained breath and breaks into a run, shoving people aside.

"Move," he yells at them.

I can only hang limply and watch as Levi's body disappears inside the alpha's house. Kari follows without a backward glance.

She's the enemy now.

If I live to face her.

The story continues in
To Kiss A Wolf

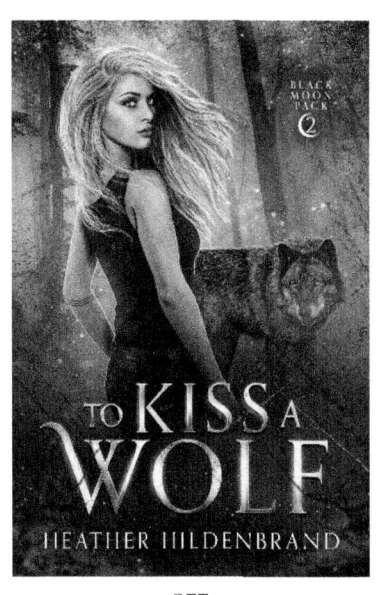

About the Author

Heather Hildenbrand lives in coastal Virginia where she writes paranormal and urban fantasy romance with lots of kissing & killing. Her most frequent hobbies are truck camping with her goldendoodle, talking to her plants, and avoiding killer slugs.

You can find out more about Heather and her books at www.heatherhildenbrand.com.

Or find her here:
- Facebook
- Facebook reader group
- Instagram
- Subscribe to her Newsletter
- Patreon

Also by Heather Hildenbrand

To Hunt A Wolf

To Kiss A Wolf

To Keep A Wolf

Midnight Bewitched

Midnight Cursed

Midnight Claimed

Wolf Cursed

Wolf Captive

Wolf Chosen

Wolf Revealed

A Witch's Call

A Witch's Destiny

A Witch's Fate

A Witch's Soul

A Witch's Prophecy

A Witch's Hope

Twisted Tides

The Girl Who Cried Werewolf

The Girl Who Cried Captive

The Girl Who Cried War

The Winter Witch

The Spring Witch

A Witch's Heart

Midnight Mate

Goddess Ascending

Goddess Claiming

Goddess Forging

Kiss of Death

Knock Em Dead

Death's Door

Dead to Rights

Dead End

The Girl Who Called The Stars

The Girl Who Ruled The Stars

Alpha Games

Alpha Trials

Alpha Chosen

Dirty Blood

Cold Blood

Blood Bond

Blood Rule

Broken Blood

One Hour: bonus novella

Imitation

Deviation

Generation

Guarded by the Alpha

Alpha Undercover

Mated to the Wilde Bear

The Bear's Fated Mate

Protected By the Bear

The Badge and the Bear

Tragic Ink: A Havenwood Falls story

Contemporary Romance

Risking My Heart

Betting My Heart

O Face

Heather also writes contemporary romcom under the name Moxie Rose. Find out more about her books at moxierosebooks.com.

Quarantine Crush

Corporate Crush

Printed in Great Britain
by Amazon